6/08

DUSSSIE

DUSSSIE

NANCY SPRINGER

WALKER & COMPANY
NEW YORK

First published in the United States of America in 2007 by
Walker Publishing Company, Inc.
Distributed to the trade by Holtzbrinck Publishers

For information about permission to reproduce selections from
this book, write to Permissions, Walker & Company,
104 Fifth Avenue, New York, New York 10011

Library of Congress Cataloging-in-Publication Data
Springer, Nancy.
Dusssie / Nancy Springer.
p.   cm.
Summary: At age thirteen Dusie makes the horrifying discovery that she, like her New
York artist mother, is a Gorgon—a Greek mythological monster sprouting snakes from
her head and capable of turning humans into stone with one angry look.
ISBN-13: 978-0-8027-9649-3 • ISBN-10: 0-8027-9649-4 (hardcover)
1. Gorgons (Greek mythology)—Juvenile fiction. [1. Gorgons (Greek mythology)—
Fiction. 2. Monsters—Fiction. 3. Snakes—Fiction. 4. Self-acceptance—Fiction.
5. Mothers and daughters—Fiction. 6. New York (N.Y.)—Fiction.] I. Title.
PZ7.S76846Du 2007   [Fic]—dc22   2007002367

Visit Walker & Company's Web site at www.walkeryoungreaders.com

Book design by Nicole Gastonguay
Typeset by Westchester Book Composition
Printed in the U.S.A. by Quebecor World Fairfield
2 4 6 8 10 9 7 5 3 1

All papers used by Walker & Company are natural, recyclable products
made from wood grown in well-managed forests. The manufacturing processes
conform to the environmental regulations of the country of origin.

To Jean Naggar

DUSSSIE

ONE

Color me stupid, but I was thirteen before I understood why my mother always wore a turban. I thought it was just part of her artistic weirdness. I had no clue until my own hair turned into snakes.

Naturally this happened the morning after I got my first period, which could have waited another thirteen years in my opinion. It *so* did not enhance my mood, what with having to get up in the middle of the night and change the sheets and everything, plus cramps, plus Mom being totally sentimental and annoying, congratulating me on "becoming a woman." I barely got back to sleep before the alarm went off, and right away I started worrying about what to wear to school. See, there was this boy I liked, and everything depended on how I looked. Not that I looked like much anyway: average height, average weight (fat), average face, brown hair and brown eyes, nose in the middle, and then on top of being totally not gorgeous, I started worrying whether boys could tell when you got your period, and I felt all swollen— even fatter than usual. I did not need anymore stress as I lurched into the bathroom with my eyes barely open.

I was so sleepy I didn't notice the crawly feeling in my scalp at first. But then I heard a hissing noise. And I caught a bleary glimpse of myself in the mirror.

I woke up fast, screaming, "*Mom!*"

She came running into the bathroom in her black silk sleep turban and jammies, took a look at me, and said, "Oh." Just like that, like she'd been hoping it wouldn't happen, but now it had, so we would just have to deal with it; Mom is all about being able to handle whatever happens without complaining. "Oh, honey, I'm sorry." Not even surprised, which was pretty bizarre, considering that I had a head full of snakes.

"Mom, *do* something!" I mean, I'm a city girl. I'd never even *seen* a snake except in a zoo or on TV.

Totally freaked, I hopped around flapping my arms, wanting to rip the snakes off my head but afraid to touch them.

"Now, Dusie, calm down." But there was a shadowy look in Mom's eyes as she leaned over me. "Let me see. Garden snakes, black snakes, corn snakes—oh, no, is that a coral snake?" Leaning closer, she peered at my head as if inspecting me for dandruff. "No, thank goodness, it's just a king snake. I don't see any poisonous species."

Weirder and weirder. Like, my mom knew how to tell snakes apart? Since when?

"And I must say," she added in a different, softer tone, as if she were critiquing somebody's abstract canvas, "the colors are quite striking. Jade green, jet black, ruby, topaz, in—what a daring combination of stripes and rings. The juxtaposition—"

I stood there stunned. I mean, up till then it hadn't been a problem that Mom was all about being an Artist, with a capital A. Famous even, because she had a sculpture in the lobby of the Whitney, a life-size stone man with an expression nobody could understand— yearning, quizzical, tragic, amused? A masterpiece, anyway, kind of the Mona Lisa of sculpture.

So my mother, Euryale Gorgon, was a celebrity, always going to parties and getting in *People* magazine. They loved her because she wore lots of extreme clothes. Mom's taste and mine couldn't be more different.

Especially now. Mom was saying, "—sophisticated, Dusie. So individualistic, so unique! So original! They make quite a dramatic statement—"

"I don't *want* to make a statement!" I shrieked. Then I burst out crying.

"Dusie . . ." Mom put her arms around me, stroking my back with her strong hands. "Honey, please don't get so upset."

I sagged against her. Always, up until then, whenever Mom hugged me, I'd felt sure everything was going to be all right.

"It's not the end of the world," she murmured, patting my back. "You'll find ways to cope. Trust me."

Cope?

Like, for how long?

What if my friends found out?

Cope? Was that the best Mom could do?

Her hug was a lie. I yanked myself away from her, bawling even harder. The snakes thrashed and coiled.

I could feel their movements through my scalp right into my skull, their bones connected to my bone. I screamed again.

Mom turned stern. "Dusie, stop it."

And somebody else said, *"Dusssie, ssstop it."* A hissy voice, not Mom's, sounded right inside my head. Or, not a voice, exactly, and it didn't really speak, just kind of goosed my mind. I can't explain, but there it was. Sarcastic: *Ssstop it, Ssstupid.*

My scream spun into a screech.

Mom ordered, "Dusie, stop! It's no use having a hissy fit."

A hissy fit was exactly what the snakes were throwing, moshing on my head and hissing like mad cats, giving me the worst bad hair day in recorded history. I howled, "I can't go to school like this! Mom, you've got to *do* something! I just want to die!" Overnight I had become, absolutely, no contest, the ugliest girl in school. Make that the ugliest girl in the country. Make that the ugliest girl in the *world*.

Mom sighed. I'd never seen her look sadder, yet her voice stayed situation-normal, like the toilet had clogged or the elevators had broken down again. "All right, Dusie. You can stay home from school today. Now, wash your face and get yourself under control. I think it's time we had a little talk."

≈ ≈ ≈

It took me till mid-afternoon to calm down enough to halfway listen and start asking questions. Like, "Mom, why didn't you tell me this stuff before?"

Sitting in the apartment window, Mom just stared down at Greene Street like she needed to really study the fire escapes and pigeons and the Chinese umbrella vendor on the corner. Daylight came in gray through the February rain, and for the first time I noticed the lines on Mom's face—a beautiful face, to me, anyway. Grecian nose, jutting cheekbones, cleft chin. To anybody who was into bland blonde cover girls, Mom probably looked ugly, but to me, she was the rock-solid, most perfect person in the world, like a goddess—

Whoa. She *was* a goddess, kind of. I'd just found out she was immortal. Several thousand years old. Those were lines of time on her face.

Her voice low, she said, "I thought—the snakes—I was hoping it wouldn't happen to you, too."

Silence, except for taxicabs and delivery vans beeping below. Slumping on the sofa, I closed my eyes.

Mom said, "Your father was mortal. You're half-human."

Half-human? And here I'd been going around thinking I was, you know, normal. Like, okay, my best friend Stephe was half-Hungarian and my other best friend Keisha was half-black, but half-human? Nobody went around being only half-human.

What if somebody found out about me?

Oh, God, it was too much to think about all at once.

Mom was saying, "You are a lot like your father. So I hoped maybe . . ." Her voice trailed off.

She was the one who had mentioned my father! Maybe, now that the secrets were coming out . . . ? Keeping my voice soft, I gave it a try. "Who was my father?"

But no go. She just shook her head and said, "He was very brave."

That was Mom's highest praise, *brave*—she was sooo all about being a strong person. It was also her standard answer whenever I asked about my father. We'd been through this many times before, although considering what I now knew, I was beginning to understand why I had no father. Before, I had been clueless. Mom's name hadn't meant a thing to me. I mean, who knows what a gorgon is anymore? Mom hadn't told me until today that under the turban her hair was vipers, under the polish her fingernails were bronze, under the caps her teeth were fangs. She hadn't told me that she'd had wings surgically re-moved by a doctor who could be blackmailed to keep quiet. She *had* told me, years ago, that she'd named me after her dead sister, but she hadn't told me that Dusie was a nickname—short for Medusa.

"Could you eat something now?" Mom asked.

"No." Eat? Was she totally crazy? Couldn't she see there were snakes on my head? Quiet snakes now, but I could feel their weight, I could feel them lazily coil-ing, I could feel their slithery length against my neck and temples, and I could just barely stand it.

"Mom," I begged, "can't we cut them off?"

Like dark, distant echoes deep inside my mind, the voices that were not voices spoke to each other:

She'sss kind of ssstupid, said one.

But sssweet, came a gentler reply.

Sssweet? She hatesss usss.

Shaking her head, looking tired, Mom was saying, "I've tried that myself, honey. I've tried cutting them off, burning them off, freezing them off, eating them off with acid, like warts . . . but they just grow back again. Instantly. Longer and thicker."

"But there *has* to be a way—"

"There's not, honey. I've tried everything."

I jumped up with a wail, and my snakes started squirming and hissing as I yelled, "*Why?*"

"Because they're the curse of Athena, sweetie. They're a fate. They're *our* fate. And that's the way fate is."

"I hate fate!" My eyes stung, but I didn't have any tears left.

"You learn to make the best of it," Mom said, her tone as gray as the rainy New York City day.

Right. Sure.

"Troubles make us strong." Mom sounded dead, but then she looked at me and I saw her force herself to lighten up. "I've started thinking of my serpents as pets," she said, smiling all bright and shiny like a steak knife. "I named one of them after Athena, actually. Then there are Hera and Demeter and—"

"Mom, stop it."

I said this even before a small, snide voice inside my head remarked, Ssstupid namesss.

Goddesss namesss, another one agreed.

Goddesssesss she hatesss.
She hatesss usss, too.

Just then Mom stood to face me. With her bravest smile she said, "Would you like to see them, honey?" She lifted her hands toward her turban.

"*No!* You're disgusting!" Snakes flailing, I jumped up, ran for my room, and slammed the door.

≈ ≈ ≈

After school Keisha phoned to ask why I'd been absent from school, but I couldn't talk. I knew I'd cry if I tried to talk, so Mom took the call on my cell phone and told Keisha I was sick. Same with Stephe, which is pronounced "Steve" even though she's a girl. Katie called, too. And the other Catie, the one with a C. And Hunter, who by the way is half Australian. Mom told them all I was sick. So they started text-messaging me GWS—get well soon?—and gon 2 DLA 2 bad U cant.

Yeah. Too bad.

I felt so cruddy I didn't text back. I slumped around thinking about how my friends were going to DLA, Dance Lights and Action, without me, and I would not have thought it was possible for things to get any worse, but of course they did. By evening, the chatter in my head sounded like tourists at Rockefeller Center. My snakes had stopped being shy and were getting acquainted. I wanted to watch TV or a movie, anything to forget about being a reptile sanctuary, but all I could hear was snake yada yada.

Hope thisss half-human hatchling will eat sssomething sssoon.

I'm hungry, too. What I wouldn't give for a nice fat field moussse.

Uncomfortable being crowded like thisss. I'm not the sssort to hisss in a pit, myssself.

They bear live young.

How awful. Why can't they lay eggsss like . . .

. . . or a tasty ssshrew. Or even a hamsssster. Any rodent . . .

Yada yada yada, hiss hiss hiss. Up until then I had kind of forgotten about hearing slithery voices in my mind. I mean, when a person has snakes on her head, a little strangeness *in* the head doesn't make much of an impression. At first I'd thought it was my imagination.

But it wasn't. I was hearing snake voices. Or not voices, exactly, but snake thoughts. Somehow their brains were hooked into my brain—well, no wonder, since their spines were sprouting out of my *skull*—

and since I think in English, I was hearing them that way. In words, but majorly weirded. Once I started to pay attention, it scared me, it was so—so not me. Not even human. Like there were smells to the thoughts: moss, frog, earthworm, leaf loam, musk. And the smells were tastes, but the tastes had colors. Greenish, brownish, scarlet, flickering forked-tongue black. It was way strange.

... *jussst a common colubrid, of no dissstinction* ...

... *hungry* ...

I'm a black racer, not a blacksssnake.

... *sssalamandersss under the ssstones by the ssstream.*

... *golden ssstripesss* ...

... *russstle my tail in the dry grasss and ssstrike* ...

... *baby pigeon crushed in my coilsss* ...

Blah blah blah, yada yada yada, hiss hiss *hiss*. I couldn't stand it. I screamed, "Shut up!"

In the sudden silence the TV sounded very loud. Paying bills at her glass-and-chrome desk in the corner—Mom decorated the way she dressed, artsy and extreme—she jumped in her corkscrew chair, swiveling to stare at me.

No need to vibrate usss, someone in my mind declared peevishly.

Mom said, "Dusie, just turn it off if—"

"Not the tube. The stupid snakes."

A coldly regal voice said in my mind, *We prefer to be addresssed as ssserpentsss.*

"I would prefer if you would *shut up!*"

I heard a hissy murmur from the crowd, and the regal one said, *Be polite. We bite.*

Ooooh, I just wanted to kill them. All of them. My fists clenched, and my mouth opened to tell them off, but I saw Mom peering at me. "Dusie?"

"They're talking at me inside my head, Mom!"

"I beg your pardon?"

Right away I knew I had made a mistake. I mean, I was assuming her snakes did the same, but from the expression on her face, nuh-uh. And there are some things you shouldn't let your mom find out. Like, I don't know, if you got a tattoo on your butt, that might be one. Or if you're hearing what should have been your hair yakking inside your mind.

"You're hearing *voices*?" Mom exclaimed.

I mumbled, "It's just the stupid snakes."

Ssserpentsss, somebody on my head objected. I ignored them.

In a too-sweet voice Mom was saying, "But, Dusie, honey, snakes don't talk."

"I *know* that."

"But you're hearing voices in your mind?"

I rolled my eyes. "Mom, forget it, okay? I'll handle it."

"But sweetie, if you're having, um, a mental episode, it might be due to, um, a chemical imbalance due to, ah, hormones. I'd better make you an appointment to see—"

"Mom, no!" As if things weren't miserable enough.

"To see a specialist."

"Mom, I'm *fine!*" Well, as fine as anybody could be with snakes for hair.

"That's for the doctor to decide, Dusie."

Oh. Just. Great. But I felt too worn out to put up a good fight.

Sssee what happensss when you fusss? said my most unfavorite voice. They were such—such *creeps*. I hated them. I wanted to smack somebody, but I was too tired. All I could do was wrap a very big, very thick towel around my head and go to bed.

TWO

In the morning, I made Mom get up before dawn. There I was, miserable and wide awake, so why should I let her sleep? I'd been trying to think what to do, and what I'd come up with was to make her cover my snakes all over with facial mud so they would look like dreadlocks—okay, really disgusting dreads, not soft like Keisha's, but at least maybe I could go to school? Not that I loved school so much, but at that point I really needed to at least pretend I was normal, not half-human and definitely not a junior Medusa. I guess I was being stupid, not facing the facts, but I felt like everything would be okay if I could just act like it was. Go do everyday things. Be with my friends.

I still hadn't eaten, I hadn't been able to sleep

much, and I felt like a zombie. My snakes acted like they were hibernating. "If you stay calm, so will they," Mom said, slathering mud on them like it was something she did every day.

"Mom, I *know*." Like I needed her telling me stuff at six o'clock in the morning?

"How would you know?"

"I'm not stupid!"

Mom didn't like being vertical at six A.M. any more than I did. "You know so much, you do this yourself from now on," she grumbled, slapping mud onto my head.

"No way."

"Yes way."

"I'm not touching them."

"Yes, you are. I'm not doing it for you after today. Wear my turbans if you're so squeamish."

"Ew!" Not her turbans, never my mother's turbans. I tied my biggest do-rag over my dreads, looked in the mirror, and felt an urge to flush myself down the toilet. I didn't even bother with makeup; what was the use? I just gulped down a bowl of Frosted Flakes, stuffed Kotex and some spare mud into my backpack, then left.

I felt so ugly I took the subway, and I hated every

woman on there with hair, even the greasy-headed
bag ladies. I felt so low I wanted to stay underground,
but I got off at my stop. Seeing homeless people huddled on the platform didn't make me feel any better.
I climbed the stairs, ducked into a narrow back street
nobody used, and tried to sneak toward my middle
school.

I never made it.

Before I got halfway there a male voice said,
"Hey, cool hair."

I turned, and oh, God, it was the boy I liked, the
tall one with eyes the color of tarnished silver, walking up to stand beside me. My heart started pounding,
and I felt crawlies on my scalp, oh no, snakes starting
to rouse. I had to calm down fast. Right now. It
wasn't like I could ever have a boyfriend anyway, not
with a head full of snakes. Forget flirting, forget dat-
ing. Forget soft kisses. Forget all those dreams of true
love.

Calm. Had to be calm. I managed to act bored
and say, "Oh, hi, Troy."

"Oh, hi, Dusie," he mimicked. "Aren't you somebody. New hairdo go to your head?" He grinned,
teasing, and suddenly his hand shot out to yank
my hair.

Only it wasn't hair. It was snakes.

He was just trying to make me giggle and squeal, but I jumped away. "Don't!"

"Why not?" He tried again.

Because I couldn't let him find out about me, that was why not. I yelled, "Get *off!*" and whacked his hand down, but that just made him laugh, like it was a game, and he grabbed for my head again.

I blocked him with both arms. "Troy, it's not funny! Let me alone!"

One of the creeps on my head, in my head, whatever, sounded a warning. *Sssevere vibrationsss.*

Predator! another one of them cried.

Yet another hissed, *Prepare to ssstrike!*

Trying to ignore them, I walked away from Troy, but he followed me, and that pissed me off. I mean, recent events had put me in sooo not a very good mood anyway.

Apparently my head residents didn't appreciate being followed any more than I did. Their voices got louder and more urgent.

Ssstalker!

Prepare for ssself-defenssse!

Someone else chimed in. *Musssk!*

Deploy musssk! Deploy fecesss! Their loud brown thoughts *smelled* like snake musk, which believe me did not improve my mood.

I had to keep looking over my shoulder at Troy, to make sure he wasn't getting too close to my "hair," and he grinned.

"What's the matter, Dusie?" he teased.

"You're ugly, that's what!" I said just because he wasn't.

"Ooooh, that's *harsh!*"

"Get away from me!"

"Hey, I'm just going to school." He kept grinning and kept following.

The snake chorus crescendoed, darker and darker. *Ssswell necksss! Musssk! Cannot deploy musssk! Cannot deploy fecesss! No tail, no cloaca! Ssshhh! Forget musssk! Present necksss! Flatten necksss! Prepare to—*

I told Troy, "Go away and let me alone!"

"What if I don't want to?" And he grabbed me. By my right wrist, as his other hand shot toward my "hair" again.

That did it.

Without even thinking, or maybe letting my headful of creepy crawlies think for me, with my left hand I snatched off my do-rag. Flakes of face mud fell all around me as my snakes reared and showed their colors, threatening, hissing, spitting.

Troy turned white, dropped my arm like it burned his hand, and took a step back, screaming, "What the—talk about ugly!"

He never got to say any more. If looks could kill . . . but mine could. I didn't realize in time, but I felt it happen as anger blazed in me, my snakes thrashed and struck at the air, my eyes flared fire, and Troy . . . Troy turned to white stone.

≈ ≈ ≈

"Did anyone see you?" Mom demanded.

"How should I know? I just pushed him over, rolled him into the alley, and ran." In other words, I'd panicked. Even now, at home, with the apartment door locked behind me, I was still pretty much hysterical. I kicked the sofa, then yelled, "Ow!" and burst out crying. I felt awful. Troy. Dead. Or petrified, whatever. Just for trying to yank my hair.

On/in my head, some snake said to another snake, *We sssaved her.*

She hasss to like usss now, another one agreed.

I did not like. Not. Like. Snakes on my head. I must never go snake-crazy again. I must never do the killer look to anybody again. Never. I had to make sure not to let it happen ever again. Never never never.

I wailed at Mom, "Why didn't you *tell* me not to turn people to stone?"

"I was hoping . . . I thought . . ." Her voice shook. She spun around and ran to the kitchen and hurried back with black plastic garbage bags; they rustled in her grip because her hands were shaking, too. "They're such *little* snakes," she managed to say, "I didn't think you could. Or I was hoping you couldn't. You're half-human." She grabbed her coat, stuffing the garbage bags into her pockets. "Wrap something around your head," she ordered, "and come on. We have to go get him before . . ."

She didn't say before what, and I didn't ask, just grabbed one of her silk scarves out of the coat closet, tied it over my snakes, and followed her. On the street, she got us a cab. We perched in the backseat. I dried my face on my sleeve, sniffled, and tried to calm down. Mom stared straight ahead.

"It's probably okay," she said softly after a while. "In New York, most people just blink and keep walking."

I knew it was not okay and it never would be okay.

"I've been through this before," Mom went on. "If anybody notices, they'll think it's something that fell off a truck. A garden gnome. Or somebody's art project."

She was trying to help. But she wasn't helping.

She had always been, like, my rock. Kind of a strict, old-fashioned rock—well, duh, she *was* way old, and so are rocks—but solid.

But now my thoughts were making me feel as if I could never trust her again.

"Your sculptures," I said after a while, running some of them through my mind: *Gladiator, Celtic Elk Hunter, Napoleonic Fusilier, Spartan Warrior,* to name only a few in her Attacker series—the critics were always talking about how startlingly vital they were, coming at the viewer with weapons as if to kill, all so lifelike—*Spartan Warrior* with actual sword wounds, *Gladiator* with whip scars—done with what the critics called "nearly supernatural authority," as if she had been there . . .

Well, she *had* been there. Hundreds of years ago.

And I knew now how the "artworks" had happened, and even to me my voice sounded dead. "Your sculptures. All so realistic. All in stone."

"Hush," Mom said.

I couldn't hush. All of a sudden I hated her. I mean really, really hated her, because when I was a little girl I'd wanted to grow up to be just like her, but now—since "becoming a woman"—ow, it hurt. "Where are we going to take Troy?" I demanded. "To your studio?"

"Yes."

"Oh, *lovely*. Are you going to exhibit him? Give him a title? 'Schoolboy Stricken with Horror of Hideous—'"

"Stop it," Mom ordered, and even though it wasn't time yet, she signaled the cab driver. "Let us out here."

I managed to keep my mouth shut until she'd paid him and he drove away.

Then I demanded, "How many people have you—"

"*Stop it*, Dusie."

We strode, hurrying, through the hardest, grayest place I'd ever been to. Hard gray street and hard gray sidewalk in the cold shadow of gray buildings under a gray winter sky.

In a gray voice Mom said, "I've managed not to—not to lose control for centuries now. The sculptures are from long ago; I keep them in storage and bring one out when I need a new work."

My mother had been lying to me. All my life. She'd let me think that while I was in school she spent her days at some studio somewhere, chipping away like Michelangelo, when really . . . really she was a serial killer, sort of.

"Most of them deserved it," she added, glancing at me, hard-eyed.

"Mom!" Suddenly I was almost crying. "Mom, no!"

"I'm not a *murderer,* sweetie. It just happened. Usually to some thug who was trying to kill me. The 'Attackers' are just enemies I had stashed away. A couple of dozen in the last four thousand years; that's not so bad."

"*Sure* it's not."

"Merciful heavens, honey, when I was your age, the king of Gaul used to kill more people than that on an average day before breakfast."

Was she a murderer? If it was self-defense? Was *I* a murderer? Maybe not exactly, even though I felt like I was. I mean, I hadn't known what was going to happen at the time. It was basically an accident, manslaughter or something.

We sssaved you, complained a snake inside my head.
Show sssome gratitude, added another.

"Shut up, creeps," I told them. I hated them; I hated everything—*why* hadn't Mom warned me what might happen?

I knew the answer to that one: because she hadn't wanted me to know about—about her.

Because she didn't want me to know what she was. And what she wasn't.

The more I thought about it, the worse I felt. We rushed along hard sidewalks leading deeper and deeper into confusion, and I just stared at the concrete. I felt so hopeless.

Finally we reached a corner near my school. Flashing lights—red, blue, white, yellow—caught my eye.

I looked up.

And almost screamed. Mom grabbed my wrist, stopping me where I stood and silently warning me to be quiet, her fake fingernails digging into my skin.

So I just stared—at two NYPD cruisers with their light bars blinking. And a rescue truck. And an ambulance with *its* flashers going. All pulled up zigzag at the mouth of the alley where I'd dumped Troy.

"Is that where . . ." Mom whispered.

I nodded.

"Too late," she breathed. "Somebody must have seen."

I stood there as if Troy had turned *me* to stone.

"Come on. We don't want them to notice us." Mom tried to tug me away.

But just then some guy let out a yell from inside the alley. Even half a block away, we could hear him. "This thing has air going in and out of its mouth!" he shouted.

Mom gasped. I whammed both hands over my own mouth to keep from screaming out loud.

"What the hell?" one of the cops yelled back. "It's just a stone—"

"It's stone, all right, but its mouth is open and it's breathing. I can feel the air moving. Get the ambulance over here!"

"You're crazy."

"No, he's not," said a different voice, a medic, maybe. "There's a heartbeat. This thing is alive!"

≈ ≈ ≈

By evening I felt so schizo glad, sad, mad, bad, and scared I had turned off my cell phone so my friends couldn't call anymore to tell me about What Had

Happened—I couldn't handle talking with anybody, not even Keisha or Stephe. I couldn't stand to watch the news anymore, either. It was *so* all about Troy, who was lying in NYU Medical Center with a dozen specialists trying to figure out what was the matter with him.

"Mom, can we turn it off?"

". . . hospital spokesperson has now confirmed," the anchorwoman was saying breathily, "that SoHo teenager Troy Lindquist has suffered some unknown disease, accident, foul play, or possibly even terrorist attack that has partially turned him to stone. While the mysterious incident has left his internal organs functioning normally, externally his entire body is now composed of a porous form of white marble, leaving him unable to move, eat, speak, or . . ."

I'd heard it a dozen times. "Mom? Off? Please?"

Perched beside me on the sofa, leaning toward the TV, she shook her head. "Not until I'm sure nobody saw you."

"Look, they *said*—"

"I know."

They had actually interviewed the kids. Friends of Troy's on their way to school had recognized the "statue" lying in the alley. When Troy hadn't showed up for homeroom, they had told the teacher, and she'd thought they were talking about a body or something, so she'd called 911.

". . . stone clothing and shoes inseparable from the stone of his skin," the anchorwoman was saying. "His fingernails, hair, and eyes also appear to have been turned to stone. While it is assumed he cannot see, his brain scan indicates heightened mental activity. There is no indication yet as to whether his condition might be contagious or criminally induced. The mayor is assembling a special task force to determine the cause of this unusual circumstance, and meanwhile, the governor is urging citizens to stay calm—"

"Mom, please." I wasn't staying calm. I started to shake again, like I'd been doing off and on since the "incident." One minute I'd feel *so* glad and thankful that Troy was still alive, which Mom said had never happened in her case. She thought it must be because I was half-human that I hadn't completely turned him to stone, just petrified his outer layer. But then the next minute I'd feel awful, because how was Troy supposed to live like that?

I mean, they had drilled holes in him for tubes to feed him and stuff, and he couldn't even blink his blind eyes to show whether he knew what was happening. Poor Troy, they *had* to find a way to make him better.

But then—this was what scared me—if they *did* help him and he got better, what would he tell them?

If they found out about me, what would they do to me?

I trembled so hard the sofa shook.

Now the TV screen showed a middle-aged man and woman with rainy gray faces. "The afflicted teenager's parents have agreed to be interviewed."

I closed my eyes and hid behind my hands.

What'sss the matter with her? a snaky voice complained in my head. I felt crawly movements on my scalp—but also a movement beside me as Mom reached for the remote and killed the TV.

Silence, except for the ragged sounds of my own sobbing. I hadn't even realized I was crying.

Mom put her arms around me, but I stiffened and pulled away.

Mom's arms fell into her lap like I'd shot them down.

Silence.

Then, in her most controlled voice, "It's not your fault, honey," Mom said.

"I don't care." I wanted to tell her it was all *her* fault, actually, but I didn't. "I've got to help him."

Isss she crazy? somebody hissed in my mind.

Mom said, "You can't. Dusie, have some sense. You can't let them find out about us."

Us.

Oh. Oh, my God.

If they took me away, they'd take Mom, too.

No. *No.* None of this could possibly be happening.

But it was.

As if something were choking me, I could barely talk. I whispered, "But, Mom, I have to do *something*—"

"What can you possibly do that will make any difference for that boy?"

I shook my head. I had no idea.

"Dusie, look at me," Mom said.

When Mom told me to do something and she really meant it, I couldn't *not* do it. And this was one of those times when she meant it. So I faced her.

My mother. Like a classical sculpture. But not

stone. All too alive, with deep, deep eyes. Something in those depths I could not read.

"Dusie," Mom told me, "You have to accept the way things are for you now. You'll come to see the good side. Being my daughter, you have a very long life to look forward to."

Oh, *terrific*. "Look *forward?*" I almost screamed. "Putting people in the hospital? With snakes on my head?"

"Honey, you'll learn to cope with your—"

I put my hands over my ears, loathing her. She wasn't a great sculptor. She wasn't anything she'd let me believe she was. Her whole life was a humongous lie. She wasn't even—*my mother* wasn't even *human*. I hated her worse than ever, yet I needed her so bad I couldn't stand it.

I jumped up and stamped my foot so hard it hurt. "Mom," I begged, "what are we going to do?"

But I already knew she had no answers for me. Because she wasn't my perfect parent anymore.

Sure enough, she said, "I don't know."

"Mom—"

"Sweetie, I don't know. I never had a daughter before." A tear rolled from each eye. And Mom never cried. Never. But never say never. "All those years," she said, "and I never had a child."

"Please," I whispered, because she had always been so strong, her pain hurt me even more than I was hurting already.

"I think we need to go to the Sisterhood," she said.

THREE

At midnight we strode into Central Park. "Don't be afraid," Mom told me.

"Of what?"

She didn't answer, just kept walking. She was wearing an emerald silk gown and a matching head-dress that framed her Greek-goddess face. I just wore a thin scarf over my snakes, and they coiled close to my scalp—because of the cold, I guess. I mean, I'm a city girl, and what I knew about snakes was mostly from horror movies, but it seemed to me I'd heard something about snakes sunning themselves. They were reptiles, not like me, and they didn't do cold very well, apparently. They were finally silent.

"Don't be afraid of what?" I insisted, so bummed I didn't really care; I just wanted to argue. "Gangs?"

But Mom actually chuckled. "Testosterone-prone youths are the last thing we have to worry about."

"Unless they're carrying mirrors and swords," said another voice. By the pale light of a thin moon, I saw a tall woman step out from between the trees to walk on the footpath by my side.

I said, "Hi, Aunt Stheno."

"Sis, I don't want to hear another word about mirrors and swords," said my mother in knife-edged tones. "Get over it."

"I'll never get over it! The three of us living peaceably at the very end of the known world, minding our own business, and that Perseus comes after us like—"

"I don't want to hear it!" Mom barked.

"Dusie has a right to know." Aunt Stheno stopped walking and grabbed my arm, turning me to face her. "Like a trophy hunter on safari, that's what, and for no reason except that we were accursed to be ugly. 'Ew, Gorgons, let's go hunt them,' as if it were the same as bagging a warthog or a rhino. Kill a Gorgon, take the head home to Athena. He—"

"Stheno," said Mother with iron in her voice, "that is *enough*."

Aunt Stheno turned away and strode on. "Hurry up. They'll be waiting," she grumbled.

She and Mom walked so fast I had to trot to keep up, as they led me along a winding path to a secret place between three giant boulders. There they stopped. Looking around, at first I saw nothing except the zigzag silhouette of the Dakota building in the distance, rocks all around and bare trees holding the sickle moon in their twiggy fingers.

"Greetings, Medusa," said a voice overhead. I looked up and gasped as an angel, no, a monster—a birdwoman—flew in and thumped down to stand beside me on scaly clawed feet that would have looked better on an ostrich. "Sorry," she told me, seeing that she had frightened me. "I don't get much chance to fly anymore. Daytime, I—"

"Greetings, Medusa," interrupted a honeyed growl from atop a nearby craggy stone. I jerked around to look. A woman's head stared at me with glittering topaz eyes, her chin resting on her—paws. Great golden, clawed paws. Lion paws.

Even before I felt Mom's knuckles nudge me in the back, I knew that this was what I was supposed to not be afraid of. "Greetings, Sphinx," I said shakily.

A ripple of womanly laughter, approving and amused, washed around me. On top of another boulder I saw something with the head and arms and breasts of a woman but the body of a huge, thick snake. Atop a third boulder I saw a woman standing on all fours, her hands serving as forelegs, her haunches those of a dragon. And flying down out of the crescent moon came another birdwoman, this one with spiky white feathers around her neck. And then another, spreading black wings, and more, landing on the rocks or standing between the trees until I lost track of how many, until I heard my mother saying, "Are we all here?"

"Siren can't make it. She has a gig," somebody said.

"She's a nightclub singer," Mom said to me, and then she started making introductions as if this cold, moonlit hill were our living room and I had walked in while she was having some friends over. "Everyone, I'd like you to meet my daughter. Dusie, sweetheart, take your scarf off." She wanted them to see the evidence, I guess. Pressing my lips together to keep from saying anything rude, I yanked the covering off my head, but my snakes just huddled on my scalp, cowering. Which was pretty much what I felt like doing at the time.

"Everyone, this is my daughter, Medusa," Mom announced. She turned to me. "Honey, you've already met Sphinx—she's a Grecian sphinx, not Egyptian, and she's a Broadway consultant. And here are the Lamia sisters." Mom nudged me toward the serpent woman and the dragon woman, both of whom nodded at me. "They are performance artists. It's not a coincidence that we're all here in New York; many of us are members of the artistic community."

I heard Aunt Stheno mutter, "As if I'm a sculptor?" Aunt Stheno worked as a bookkeeper. But all of a sudden I realized that probably some of Mom's "works of art" were really Aunt Stheno's petrified people. I mean, she used to do it, too, right?

Or maybe—maybe she still did?

"Stop," I whispered to myself, feeling like I couldn't take much more.

Mom continued as if she hadn't heard. "The Eumenides sisters. Nemesis is a member of the American Academy of Poetry." Turning to me again, she smiled at the winged woman who had landed first, and I winced again at the sight of those big, scaly bird feet with thick gray claws.

She must have seen me looking, because she said, "It's amazing what you can hide under a caftan." Her voice was ancient, as dry and warm as bones bleaching in the desert sun.

I blushed so hotly that my snakes squirmed. "Um, excuse me," I whispered.

"Not at all, little daughter. Take a good look, and be grateful for your own pretty feet."

"And be grateful you don't have wings," added the Lamia with the dragon tail and, yes, bat wings.

Several voices agreed that wings were the worst. "Almost impossible to hide them," said the other Lamia, the anaconda look-alike.

"And *feathers*," said the birdwoman with the spiky white ruff. "What a curse, how they itch."

"Your snakes will itch only when they shed their skins," Aunt Stheno told me kindly.

"At least none of her snakes are poisonous," said Mom.

"Good!" said Nemesis. "Little Medusa, be grateful—"

I felt grateful for nothing and I could not stand to hear another word of this. I yelled, "Stop it!"

They fell silent, except for Mom, who said, "Dusie, we're just trying to help."

"I don't want help to be a freak!"

Freak! Freak! Freak, echoed away between the rocks

before a honeyed growl said, "What *do* you want, daughter of Gorgon?"

I turned to the Sphinx with Mom's warning fingers nudging my back. No need. I couldn't speak.

The Sphinx said, "You would rather be such a freak as Aphrodite, perhaps? Or Athena?"

My mouth opened twice before I managed to whisper, "They're still around?"

"Of course. They're immortals, too."

"But—but where?"

"Hollywood."

In a voice like asphalt Nemesis said, "No substantial poetry comes out of them."

I felt the glittering gaze of the Sphinx on me, even though I couldn't bear to look directly at her as she said, "They are freaks, too. They are freaks of beauty, that is all. And I am here to tell you, Medusa, there is more to becoming a woman than being pretty. I ask you again: what is it that you want?"

By the chill in my spine and the coiled stillness of my snakes I knew I had to answer. "I—I want Troy to be okay again."

They all knew what had happened. I'd heard Mom on the phone, filling them in when she'd called the meeting.

"You are concerned with the fate of the boy?" The Sphinx sounded sublimely indifferent. "Why?"

"Because I don't want to hurt people!"

"She is half-human," Mom said from behind my back. "She has compunction. She feels she has done something wrong."

"Nonsense," said the Sphinx in the same tone, ancient and stony. "Conscience has nothing to do with us, little Medusa. Forget the boy. He can do you no harm."

"But what if . . ."

"No ifs. Remember, I am the Sphinx, and I know. He will lie there without speaking until he grows old and dies."

I felt a chill like a desert night falling.

"Dismiss him from your mind, young Medusa," the Sphinx went on. "I asked you what you *want*. Before any of this happened, what was the deepest wish of your heart?"

And I thought: Troy. . . .

Forget soft kisses. Forget all those dreams of true love.

Tears stung my eyes as I blurted out the truth. "I want someone . . . like him, a boy, I mean . . . someone special."

"She wants a sweetheart," someone whispered, and a murmur went around the Sisterhood.

"That's what we all want."

"Kind eyes and a warm heart."

"She just wants love, that's all."

"True love."

Yes. Yes, that special love was what I had always dreamed of. I knew I wasn't worthy yet, but if I could learn enough about clothes and makeup and how to act, if I could grow pretty enough, then maybe someday—

The Sphinx spoke, her lioness voice gentler. "But in this, too, we can help you, little daughter."

My dream shattered like glass breaking. Freaks, calling me daughter? I wanted to scream, stamp my feet, hit something. My mind went red with rage so fiery it warmed my snakes and woke them. I felt them rear, heard them hissing like ticked-off alley cats. I snaked my neck as I swung around, peering at a circle of monster women in the dark. "Look at you!" I cried at all of them. I turned on my mother. "Look at *you!* What a life, hiding your snakes, your teeth, your nails, pretending to be normal. Well, you're not. You're not even a real sculptor. You're a fake. You're a poser."

In a tone so steely that I knew I had hurt her, she said, "I am a *real* gorgon."

"Well, I don't want to be a gorgon!"

If "becoming a woman" meant growing up to be another one of—of my Mom—no. *No.* I felt like I *had* to hurt her, to get away from her. I felt like I was fighting for my life. "I don't want to be like you! Any of you!" I yelled, glaring at all of them. "I'm not *going* to be like you!" My voice broke with the weight of emotion it carried, because nobody would ever love me now, nobody could love a monster. Unless . . .

In that moment I knew what I had to do. I said, "I am going to lose these snakes."

Silence, except for a hissy sort of tee-hee-hee inside my head. My snakes were laughing.

"I mean it." There had to be a way to get rid of them. And I would find it. I would make it happen.

I would do it. Even though my rage had whooshed out of me and left me trembling, even while the snakes quivered with laughter on my head, I knew bone-deep that I needed to keep trying until I found a way to be myself and not my mother's daughter.

"I mean it," I said again, as quiet as the moon now.

There was a sigh from the Sisterhood that felt

like "Amen." Then the Sphinx growled, and I turned to her.

As if she needed to see something inward, she narrowed her topaz eyes, her gaze heavy-lidded, shadowed. Somehow this made her even scarier than before, so fearsome that I took a step back. Yet when she spoke, her deep-chested voice came out calm, almost kind.

She said: "To lose, you must win, and to win, you must loosen, Medusa. I foresee that you will walk this way again." She opened her eyes. "Euryale, take her home."

I glanced at my mother, then stared. Under the shadow of her turban, Mom's face looked like a carving in white marble. "Sphinx, what riddle is this?" she whispered.

But the Sphinx answered only, "Bring her back when the maiden moon shines again."

And when I looked to the top of the boulder, the Sphinx was gone.

FOUR

Even though I had been up really late, the next morning when the SoHo branch library opened, there I was waiting at the door. With a big ugly babushka tied over my head, in my sloppiest old bib overalls, I stood there like a homeless person eager to get in for the day to stay out of the cold.

Only warmth wasn't what I wanted. I was there for info I couldn't find on the Internet. Surely a real library would have a book just for me. Maybe something in the hygiene section: *Eliminating Dandruff, Head Lice, and Scalp Snakes.* Or *Little-Known Side Effects of Puberty.* Or something in how-to, like *Reptile Removal for Dummies: Rid Your Head of Troublesome Serpents.*

It'sss no ussse, one of my snakes told me, sounding smug.

You're ssstuck with usss, agreed another one.

"We'll see about that," I muttered. A crazy homeless person talking to herself.

Okay, trying to be real about this, I knew I needed to know a lot more about snakes before I could even begin to figure out how to get rid of my headful. I mean, just calling an exterminator wouldn't work under the circumstances. I was going to have to come up with a plan myself, and so far, all I knew was that at least one of my snakes was hungry for crayfish. I knew this because I had actually slept for a little while the night before, and during that time I had crawled through grass and mud along a stream, stuck my head under the water, and gulped raw soft-shelled baby crayfish in my dreams. Ick.

It was Saturday morning, so there were not many people at the library yet. Kids liked to sleep in on Saturday. They wouldn't start showing up to work on their term papers till afternoon.

When the doors opened, I scuttled in without looking at anybody, heading for a computer. SEARCH BY SUBJECT: SNAKES. I managed to come up with a couple of call numbers, then headed for the stacks.

There. A whole shelf full of books on snakes.

And right in front of them stood a skinny old bony-faced man. I mean *old*. All bent over like a rusty fire escape falling down. He wore pleated pants hiked up practically to his armpits by bright red suspenders, with a starchy white shirt ballooning out around them. Totally and majorly in my way, he stood staring up from under his hunchback at the snake books.

My snake books. I needed them.

I shoved in front of the old man and started grabbing books before he could get them.

Like, *rude*. I was being so rude I thought he would move away. But he didn't. He stayed right where he was, like his big feet in their old-man leather shoes were stuck to the tile. "Goodness," he said, "you must really like snakes."

I ignored him, piling books into my arms: *The World of Snakes, The Encyclopedia of Snakes, Snakes of North America.*

"I do, too," the old man talked on, his voice warm and high and breezy like a summer sky. "I think they're fascinating creatures, the way they walk without legs and swim without fins."

I felt my snakes stir in silent approval, like cats purring without making sound.

The old man continued to talk. "Every term I audit a course at NYU, and I'm trying to decide whether to take herpetology next, or history of architecture."

But he was way too old. Surprised out of my silence, I looked at him. "You go to school?"

I guess he'd been taller once, but bent over by age, he was just my height. He nodded, gazing back at me with pale, eager eyes. "I've been taking courses every spring and fall since I retired. In twenty-two years I've taken forty-four courses."

"But . . . but what for?"

"To learn. I enjoy it. And the college kids keep me young." He smiled all over his sharp face. "Last term I took Writing Personal Poetry. I didn't do very well. The instructor said I wrote political essays that rhymed. But I had a wonderful time. Where do you go to school?"

Probably I didn't anymore. Mom had arranged for me to go see some shrink she knew on Monday, and he was supposed to let her know whether I was sane or not, but also give me a medical excuse. To Mom this was no big deal, because she didn't understand about school, or think I needed it. I mean, she was the next best thing to a goddess, so she'd learned

everything she needed to know on her own, without teachers, and for friends, she had the Sisterhood.
But me—you'd think I would be glad not to have to
go to school, but I wasn't. I mean, what was I supposed to do all day, chat on the Internet? Even if I
were allowed—which I wasn't—it just wouldn't be
the same as—friends, what was I going to tell my
friends? I still hadn't explained anything to Hunter
or Keisha or Stephe or— or anybody. I couldn't tell
them the truth, but I didn't want to lie to them, and
as far as going anyplace with them, forget it.

Was I even going to *have* any friends anymore?

I didn't answer the old guy's question. I turned
my back on him and walked away with my armload
of snake books. Rude. I felt like being rude.

"Happy reading!" he called after me.

Right. Sure.

≈ ≈ ≈

Safe at home, I threw the babushka in a corner and
grabbed myself something to eat. Actually, a lot to
eat. Two shrimp egg rolls, cold cuts, a tuna salad
sandwich, three chicken empanadas, and half a cal-
zone. I didn't know why I was so hungry.

Ra+sss, somebody in my head urged. Don't you have any sssucculent young ra+sss?

"Ick!" Okay, I *did* know why I was so hungry, but not for cereal bars or fruit salad. I was chowing down like a pregnant woman because I had to feed the snakes as well as myself. And the snakes were carnivores.

Frogsss? asked somebody else, sounding all green with longing. Newtsss?

"Listen," I complained, "I'm not an ecosystem." I finished up with some mint cookies and a dish of butter-pecan ice cream just for me. What a pig-out. I was going to be as big as a bus if I kept this up. After clearing away some of the evidence, I settled in the front room and started to read.

At first it was boring. Snakes took their body temperature from the environment. (Yawn.) Because they didn't spend their own energy keeping warm, they didn't have to eat much. (You wouldn't know it from listening to my bunch.) This made them good at living in deserts. (I wished mine would go to a desert and stay there.) Snakes could see pretty well, but they wouldn't notice you if you didn't move. (Ho-hum.) They smelled and tasted prey with their tongues. (No, duh.) They couldn't hear much, just felt vibrations. Having no external ears, snakes were about 90 percent deaf—

Right there I stopped being bored and got a real creepy feeling. Okay, my snakes could feel vibrations, but no way could they actually listen to me talking, not so as to understand the words.

Okay, I knew I was hearing their thoughts, but, color me clueless, up till then I hadn't really understood that *they* were hearing *mine.*

Not hear, Ssstupid, said the regal voice in my head. **We are your thoughtsss.**

What was that supposed to mean?

We are the dark and ssssecret cranny dwellersss of your mind.

Oh, give me a break! I threw down the book with a bang just as Mom came zipping in on her way from someplace to someplace else. What the heck did she do all day, anyway, if she wasn't sculpting statues? Where was she going in such a hurry, for a pedicure? Were her toenails bronze, too? I sooo did not feel like asking her any of this, and when I whammed my book down, she gave me a wary look. "Dusie, what was that all about?"

"Nothing."

On my head I felt the snakes—active, crawling. I'd vibrated them.

Mom asked, "What are you reading?"

"Nothing, Mom."

Mom hadn't said a word about my dissing her in front of all her freak friends, but I had a feeling she was not happy with me. Which made me feel bad, but at the same time mad at her, too. I mean, she was my mother. She was supposed to protect me. Somehow she should have kept all this from happening. She had lied to me, or at least she hadn't told me the truth. I had always looked up to her but now she had let me down, so she could just keep her distance, thank you very much.

Which she did. She went away somewhere, and I picked up another book and kept reading. Or tried to keep reading. My cell started ringing. First it was Hunter wanting to know whether I was feeling any better. I told her I just had cramps. She said I was missing all the excitement, everybody was totally freaked after what had happened to Troy Lindquist, like, was it going to happen to somebody else? I had to make an excuse and get off the phone, I felt so bad. Like, guilty. And then Catie with a C called, and Stephe, and Keisha, and I kept feeling more and more miserable. It was weird. You'd think I'd be glad to hear from my friends, but instead I felt more and more awful because I wasn't one of them anymore and they didn't even know it. They treated me the same as before, and after a while I couldn't stand it. I turned off the phone.

I couldn't read anymore, either. I just wandered around the apartment for I don't know how long. Finally, I went to Mom's bedroom and borrowed her big antique hand mirror—everything Mom owned was either ultramodern or antique, nothing in-between. I took the mirror to the kitchen table. Also a notebook, a fluorescent green gel pen, and *Snakes of North America*.

Milk snakes, corn snakes, all the snakes my mother had mentioned were North American snakes, and it would make sense if all the snakes on my head were American, so to speak, because I was. I bet all the snakes on my mother's head were Greek.

I held up the mirror by its engraved silver handle to look at my snakes, and there they all were, heads up, looking back at me. A babble of snaky voices burst out.

There she isss!

No ssscales!

I stuck out my tongue at them. They all flickered their forked tongues like mad.

She'sss tasssting usss!

She callsss that fat thing a tongue?

She'sss sssmelling usss!

She'll find out we're classsy sssnakesss!

No hognossse sssnakesss on thisss head!

No worm sssnakesss.

No low classs—

Blah blah blah, yada yada yada. I rolled my eyes.

How doesss she do that?

Enough already. I set down the mirror, opened the book, and started looking through the pictures. All the weight on my head shifted forward as the snakes looked, too, shading my face like the bill of a baseball cap.

"There's one of them," I muttered, recognizing bright red-black-yellow-black bands. I started reading.

Lampropeltisss triangulum elapssoidesss? complained the regal voice in my head. *What sssort of name isss that? I am Ssswift-Ssstrike, I am Ever-Watcher, I am Doom-Dealer. I am—*

Scarlet king snake. I should have known. I kept reading.

I have ssscales ssso sssmooth they ssseem shiny and polished, bragged the king snake, picking up the words from my mind, I guess. They were the words I was reading in the book. *I have red dorsssolateral bandsss. I can be differentiated from the poisssonousss coral sssnake by remembering the ssslogan "Red by black meansss friend of Jack." I have an undivided anal plate.*

"You don't have *any* anal plate. Unless it's buried in my head."

I am noted for my ophiophagousss inclination, he said, hesitating only slightly. He didn't know what that meant. *I* didn't know what that meant. But he was still bragging.

She, the scarlet king snake corrected me.

Sure, okay, fine, whatever. My scarlet king snake was female. I jotted some notes, then flipped pages, looking for more of my snakes.

Four hours later I was still there, and the list, with lots of scratch-outs and corrections, looked like this:

Scarlet King Snake, 1, female, bossy, look up "ophiophagous." King snakes eat small mammals, birds, fish, frogs, love turtle eggs. Ick.

Milk Snake, 1, similar to K.S., doesn't really

suck milk from cows. Whirs tail & strikes if provoked.

Eastern King Snake, 2, bright yellow & black. Robust neck and jaw muscles. If molested will bite w/ great determination. Aaagh

Corn Snake, 3, <u>docile</u>, (yay!) kept as pet, bright yellow w/ orange blobs, eats rats in corncribs

Pine Woods Snake, 1, solid amber, eats lizards, frogs, salamanders

Garter Snake, 4, it's garter, not garden, like the thing guys used to wear to hold up their socks. Striped. Hangs out by streams, eats minnows, frogs, salamanders.

Ribbon Snake, 3, gracile (?) small-headed, does not bite unless seized, when might nip firmly. 1 w/ blue stripes 1 w/ red etc. etc. getting tired of this

Black Racer, 3, noted for alert demeanor, readiness to bite, and speed. Aaagh. Climbs well. Swallows prey alive. Eats baby birds out of nests, frogs, insects etc. etc.

Blue Racer, 2, similar, dark turquoise color

Yellow-bellied Racer, 1, sage green on top, eats cicadas

Indigo Snake, 1, shiny ink blue. Lives in

burrows w/ gopher turtles. Hisses, flattens muscular neck vertically, and strikes. Oh, great, just great. Pretty, though.

"Aaaagh!" I stopped, shocked at myself, calling a snake pretty? I was supposed to be finding a way to get rid of my snakes, and here I was writing down that they ate cicadas and they were pretty.

All through this, the snakes kept gabbing like dee-jays. I was starting to learn to tune them out like background noise, like the radio or the television if somebody left it on in the next room.

I had twenty-two snakes listed so far, and I was tired and cranky but almost finished. "Okay, you other stripy ones," I muttered. Two of them, one sticking its blunt little face out from behind each of my ears. They had pretty yellow and tan stripes on their sides, but their tops were solid black. "You're not garter snakes. What are you?"

I was talking to myself, but they replied in my head. We are Quick-Flick, Sssky-Bridger, Water-Ssstrider.

Ssswift-Ssswimmer.

Crayfisssh-Killer.

I mumbled, "Crayfish," and turned to the index.

There was only one reference. Page 171. A second later I yelped, "You're queen snakes!" *Regina septemvittata.* "Are you by any chance female?"

No, they were guy queen snakes. I sensed it right away. But before they could really answer, the scarlet king snake, who *was* female, cut in.

Bearersss of live young, she sneered. *Blood-Birthersss, like mammalsss. There'sss nothing regal about them.*

I ignored her and moved on. "Okay, almost finished. You green snakes are Green Snakes, I guess?" All the snake names in the book were capitalized.

We are Hatchlingsss of the Sssun, one of them said. *We are Sharp-Sssight.*

We are Tree-Climber, said another.

They sure were, but according to the book, the Smooth Green Snake, aka grass snake, was more likely to stay on the ground and hunt crickets, caterpillars, grasshoppers, and so on. The Rough Green Snake climbed trees to hunt bugs, hanging in a loop from a branch to sleep at night.

I liked the idea of the shining green snake hanging like a hoop earring in a tree. And the book said green snakes didn't bite. Without thinking, just curious, I asked, "Are you guys rough or smooth?" and put up a hand to find out.

To touch.

I touched my snakes.

Oooh, scales, like a thousand polished, diamond-shaped fingernails, warm and cool at the same time, with strong, strong muscles rippling underneath, steely, alive. The touch zipped like an electric shock straight to my heart. I snatched my hand away, but the feel of snake tingled and lingered on my fingertips the way the feel of my first kiss, last summer, had lingered for hours on my lips.

FIVE

A big box arrived at the apartment door the next day, which was really bizarre, because it was Sunday. No mail, no UPS, no messenger service, and anyway, we hadn't buzzed anybody in. But when I opened the door to go get Mom a newspaper, there it sat.

Not cardboard. Black enameled wood, with a lid and a fancy padlock. Like a treasure chest. A hinged, arched lid with "Miss Medusa Gorgon" painted on it in curly white letters.

"Cool!" I exclaimed.

"What in the world?" Mom wondered aloud.

We dragged the box into the apartment, and of course I had to see what was in it right away. A little key hung by a jewelry chain from the padlock. I opened it.

"Hats!"

Or head coverings, anyway, lots of them, wrapped in white tissue paper. There was a big puffy-crowned hat with a ruffled brim, all royal blue crushed velvet. There was a wide-brimmed, denim hippie hat with embroidered daisies. There was a real sunbonnet like from *Little House on the Prairie*, only in posy-print electric lavender. There was a silky sort of modesty wrap like Muslim girls wear. There was a big shawl in bright-colored stripes with long, beaded fringe. There was a *Cat in the Hat* hat. There was a fake fur hat with dangling purple ermine tails. Just to mention a few.

Sssweeet, hissed one of the corn snakes. I was starting to be able to tell them apart in my head.

Looksss like a prey item, remarked a king snake.

"Shut up," I told him. His comment smelled like a gerbil cage but the fake fur hat *was* the sweetest. They were all way cool, all the hats, which was as bizarre as the box itself. What I mean is, usually when I get a present, I feel good and everything because somebody gave me something, but almost always it's the wrong color or the wrong size or just not for me, you know? But these hats were perfect. All of them.

I never would have thought of them, yet they were so me. It was like somebody was reading my mind.

And there was no card or anything to say who had sent them.

As I unpacked them, my mother watched with her eyebrows arching higher and higher until she looked like a McDonald's sign. "My sister?" she wondered aloud.

I think we both knew better, because Aunt Stheno is kind of resentful most of the time, like, she and Mom don't get along that great. But I ran for the phone anyway. "Aunt Stheno," I demanded when she answered, "are you the one who sent me a big box full of hats?"

No. No, she hadn't. She wished she could have, but bookkeepers, unlike certain famous "sculptors," don't earn that kind of money.

So much for Aunt Stheno.

After I hung up, I looked at Mom. The hats had to come from somebody who knew what I had to cover up. And my heart swelled, because I thought I had the answer. "Mom," I said, kind of choked up because I'd been feeling so hateful about her, "it was you, wasn't it?"

She shook her head. "Dusie, when was the last time I gave you anything you actually liked? No, it wasn't me."

What was I thinking? Of course my annoying mother couldn't do *anything* right.

But if it wasn't her or Aunt Stheno, who was it?

By the worry line deepening between Mom's eyes, I could tell she was wondering the same thing. Which just made me pissed at her, because the hats were great, so what did it matter where they came from, really? I stopped thinking about it, just grabbed one hat after another and tried them on in front of the full-length mirror. I settled on the blue crushed velvet hat as my absolute favorite and stood there staring at myself.

I looked almost kind of cute with the snakes covered—

Crap. No matter what I did, it was all going to be cover up, cover up, from now on. Lying all the time, pretending to be—I was so never going to be normal. Only half-human. Hiding my head, hiding my—

Guilt.

Even if I never did anything else horrible, look what I'd already done. . . .

My happy mood had evaporated, but I kept staring in the mirror, at the blue hat.

"Mom," I said without turning around, "can we go to the hospital and visit Troy?"

I heard a crash, like she'd dropped something.

"Nobody'll see the snakes if I keep my hat on," I said.

Actually I wasn't sure I would keep the hat on if I could get a minute alone with Troy. Maybe I needed to make the snakes apologize and take back what they had done to him. No, that seemed lame . . . but still, I felt like it was up to me and my snakes to help Troy somehow, in spite of what the Sphinx had said. I mean, she had sounded so doom-and-destiny sure about Troy, but she was a mythological creature and this was New York City in the twenty-first century, you know? There ought to be some way to break her rules. Or, if she wanted to run things by fairy-tale rules, wasn't I pretty much a mythological creature myself, with snakes on my head? So shouldn't there be something mythical or fairy-tale-like I could do? Go on a quest or something to save Troy? Give Troy a kiss on his stone lips, like he was Sleeping Beauty?

"Absolutely not," Mom gasped.

"But, Mom—" I turned to argue with her, but stopped when I saw her face. She had gone chalk white.

"Dusie, no. You must not go anywhere near that boy. Right now you're safe, but if anybody connects you with him . . ."

"Whatever," I mumbled.

"There's no telling what might happen. And there's nothing you can do for him anyway."

"Um . . ."

"Dusie, you are not to put yourself in danger. I mean it."

"I can tell you mean it," I grumbled. She looked scared stiff. So okay, I'd let it go. For today. And I wouldn't mention it to Mom again. But I couldn't let her run my life anymore, no matter how much she meant what she said, because look how she'd lied to me and what a mess she'd got me into. I was going to have to figure out things on my own from now on, and I *would* visit Troy. The minute I got a chance.

≈ ≈ ≈

I couldn't manage it the next day because Mom stayed home to take me to the shrink.

I heard her on the phone, telling somebody she couldn't make it to her shift at the food pantry and could they please fill in for her?

Huh. My mother did volunteer work? I guess she'd mentioned stuff like that before, helping at the homeless shelter or raising money for animal rescue, but I hadn't paid much attention. Everybody knew celebrities did charity work to look good, and I had thought she really was a sculptor, a famous one.

Whatever, because what she really is, is a gorgon. And even if she spent all day feeding homeless people, it wouldn't change that. I kept reminding myself of this, because watching her drift around the apartment with her "be strong" look on her face as she polished the glass tables and silver chrome picture frames—just for something to do— I felt scared that I might start trusting her again. I still had feelings for her in my heart, I really wanted—

But I had to remember: She was the one who had gotten me into this mess.

I made sure to keep that in mind pretty much all

day. In the apartment. In the taxi. At the doctor's office.

≈ ≈ ≈

After seeing the shrink I headed into DeLucia's Deli with my funky-colored fake fur hat on, to get me and Mom some paella with extra yellow rice and a couple of eclairs. They make the best eclairs. Anyway, the reason I mention it is that, right inside DeLucia's, at one of the cafe tables, sat the little old man from the library.

New York City being NYC, I'd assumed I'd never see him again. But there he was. Just my luck, he probably lived in my neighborhood. I noticed him right away, like, *ow*. But he didn't see me, because he was bent over his plate eating his cream of broccoli soup.

I wanted to back out the door. I'd been so rude to the old guy, I wanted to run away. Then I remembered how bad I'd felt that day, and it kind of surprised me to realize I felt way better now—maybe because my period was almost over, or because of the hats? I don't know. Anyway, feeling better kept me from ducking out the door. Instead, I walked over to him.

"Um, sir," I managed to say.

He looked up and smiled like I was his best friend.

"Um, I want to apologize," I blundered on. "I mean, I'm sorry I was such a—" I stopped myself from saying the word that came to mind. He might not appreciate it. "I'm sorry I was, um, so rude the other day—"

"That's all right. We all have those days." He had the greatest voice, correct yet breezy bright. "Sit down, sit down!" He gestured to the other chair at his table.

Why not? I sat.

"Anybody could see you were having a bad day," he said, laying his soup spoon aside. "Don't give it another thought. Did you finish your report on snakes?"

That hurt, because I missed going to school, or at least I missed seeing my friends, especially Keisha and Stephe. I mean, they were still phoning, and sending me text messages and e-mails and stuff, but what was I supposed to tell them? Hey, c'mon over; send pictures of the new me with your cell phone; I'll bead your hair and you can French braid my snakes?

So all of a sudden I was by myself almost all the time. I didn't even like to IM anymore. Being grounded drives me crazy, but this was even worse, because I was basically grounding myself. Now that I knew I was only half-human, I didn't think I could ever come out of exile. I just had too many secrets. The only ones who knew the truth were the Sisterhood, including Aunt Stheno and Mom, and I didn't want to talk with them—especially Mom—because they were freaks and they were sooo annoying and I didn't want to be like them. But I needed somebody to talk with so bad that here I was chatting with a bony old guy in a deli.

Letting him assume I had been working on a report, I nodded, and to be polite I asked, "Are you taking the herp, uh, herpes—"

"Herpetology. Study of snakes."

I nodded like sure, I knew that. "Are you taking it?"

"Herpetology class? Yes, I am. It just started this morning. Fascinating." He sat up almost straight, beaming. "The professor gave us some cultural background. Did you know that almost all ancient peoples worshipped snakes?"

My snakes must have picked up the words from my head. I felt crawlies under my hat, and in my head someone said, **Yesss!**

"They almost all had a myth of the world serpent,"

the old guy went on. "A giant serpent coiled around the world with his tail in his mouth. The rainbow was a sky-serpent drinking from the ocean. The mother goddesses wore serpents. Even to the classical Greeks, the serpent was a symbol of wisdom and healing . . ."

My snakes were hissing all sunny yellow, *Sssky sssserpent, yesss! Goddesss Demeter, healing, wisssdom, yesss!*

Next they'd be bobbing around under my hat.

"Um, I gotta go," I said, starting to get up.

The old man lifted a skinny hand to stop me. "Am I boring you? We'll talk about something else. I am curious, why are you here at this hour? Did you not have school today?"

"I don't go to school anymore," I said.

"You *don't*? An intelligent young lady like you?"

"I have a medical excuse." This was true, or it would be in a few days. Talking to the psychiatrist, I had told him quite truthfully that I heard voices in my mind coming from the snakes that were growing out of my head instead of hair. He had asked me to take off my hat and show him the snakes. I had told him I couldn't because that would kill him. Well, the

Greek mythology stuff I'd found on the Internet said a gorgon was so ugly that just looking at one would turn a man to stone. Really made *me* feel good. Although actually, Troy hadn't turned to stone just from looking at my snakes. He'd still been okay till I, you know, glared at him. If looks could kill and all that. But I felt pretty annoyed at the therapist, so I wasn't taking any chances. I had to make sure that it never happened again. Never.

So after I'd told him about the snakes and the voices, et cetera, the doctor had said I definitely needed a medical excuse from school and also a referral to a shrink specializing in adolescents. On the way home, Mom had said we'd worry about that later. One crisis at a time.

"Medical excuse?" The old man leaned closer over the deli table, giving me such a kind look that I'm sure he thought I had leukemia. I mean, he thought I had lost all my hair from chemo and that was why I wore a big hat all the time. "I'm sorry," he told me, real nice, nothing sloppy about it. "By the way, my name is Cyril Ford. Call me Cy. Rhymes with Hi." He extended his knobby old hand toward me, and I shook it. His hand felt light and dry, like driftwood. "And you are?" he asked.

"Dusie," I told him. "Dusie Gorgon."

"Dusie," he said, his pale eyes going thoughtful, like he was focusing on the name. "Dusie, and you *are* a doozy, aren't you? Nice to meet you, Dusie." He shook my hand again, then picked up his soup spoon. "May I treat you to some small token of friendship? A slice of apple pie?"

"Um, no thanks. I gotta go order paella for Mom and me." But I felt myself smiling at him as I got up to leave.

≈ ≈ ≈

Sitting cross-legged on my bed so I wouldn't have to hold the big dictionary, I looked up some words. *Gracile* meant "slender and graceful." *Cloaca* was the vent in the posterior end of a snake through which musk and feces were emitted. *Ophiophagous* meant "eating snakes."

King snakes. Ophiophagous.

King snakes ate other snakes.

I grabbed *The Encyclopedia of Snakes* and looked up king snake just to be sure. Yeppers. King snakes even ate rattlesnakes.

Wow. Gotta respect king snakes.

Then I started to get an idea.

See . . . if I didn't cut the snakes off my head myself, like, if they just sort of fell victim to natural predation, maybe they wouldn't grow back twice as big, right? Maybe they wouldn't grow back at all.

Of course, if I'd really thought about it, I would have realized that then I'd be left with four king snakes, or at least with one top-dog, gladiator, all-victorious, totally egotistic king snake. And when you've got snakes growing out of your head, just cutting down on numbers is not really an improvement. With snakes for hair, one snake is as bad as twenty-seven.

But I didn't get a chance to really think about it, because the snakes snagged the idea right out of my mind, and all the garter snakes and ribbon snakes and corn snakes and stuff started to thrash and whimper.

I'm ssscared, whined one of them, might have been the yellow-bellied racer.

Somebody else cried, *Danger! Danger in the head.*

Ssslither! Flee!

Russstle tailsss!

No tailsss!

Can't flee!

Panic, panic, dark brown musky-smelling panic, and at the same time the bigger snakes, like, the racers, whipped into a different sort of hissy fit. The indigo snake darted her body right down in front of my face. I saw all her underside scales like treads on a bulldozer for an instant before she bent like a pretzel and glared into my eyes. She startled me so bad, nose to nose with me, that I didn't even put up a hand to bat her away.

She hissed, *Shame on you!* as she swelled and flattened her neck like a cobra imitation, then struck.

It was like a tiny fist had hit the tip of my nose, except this fist had teeth and it bit me.

I yelled, "Ow!" staring cross-eyed down my own schnoz. There she hung, thrashing like a pit bull with the fleshy part of my nose in her mouth, hissing through her flattened nostrils, while at the same time twenty-some voices clamored inside my head.

Go Indigo! (black racer.)

You show her! No nonsssensssse! (pine woods snake?)

We're all on thisss head together! Yesss! We didn't asssk to be on her ssstupid head! It'sss not like we want to be here! All sssqueezed, no freedom—Can't even ssslide in the grasss—never a tassste of a grub—No matesss—And now she wants the king sssnakesss to eat usss? Bite her! Let'sss all bite her! (Impossible to identify; too many all at once.)

Also, I heard my mother's voice calling from the living room, "Dusie? Are you okay?"

And amid all the ruckus I heard the regal, bored query of the scarlet king snake: *What'sss in it for me?*

"White mice from the pet shop," I replied, surprised to find myself hoping savagely that they would stick in her gut and kill her.

I heard that! Her red, black, and yellow head flashed down and struck my cheek.

I screamed, lunged off the bed, ran to the kitchen, and yanked open the freezer compartment of the refrigerator. I stuck my head in there.

Hey! complained twenty-seven snakes.

My mother exclaimed, "Dusie, what in the world?" I heard her drop her magazine and follow me into the kitchen, but I kept my head in the freezer.

I told my snakes grimly, "Listen up, all of you creeps, or I will freeze you into Popsicles." I knew they couldn't hear me, I knew they just picked up the thoughts from my mind, but I couldn't seem to help talking aloud to them. Especially now. Between my teeth I told them, "First of all, none of you are to bite me. Ever. Never again."

The milk snake said, *Let go of her, Indigo.* Already

they sounded more sluggish. And the indigo snake did let go of me, coiling in on herself, still hissing.

"You promise me that," I continued, "and I promise I will drop the idea of siccing the king snakes on you."

We promisssse! said various voices, mostly garter snakes.

I said, "I want the biters to promise."

Behind me, Mom was saying, "Dusie, you're dripping blood on the Healthy Choice dinners!"

I ignored her except to stick my head deeper into the freezer. The scarlet king snake said frostily, *I ssspeak for all of usss. We promissse.*

Good enough. I got my head out of there and reached for a paper towel to swab my nose. Mom had gone out of the room. I heard her rummaging in the bathroom, looking for Band-Aids, probably.

I stood there with the paper towel soaking up quite a lot of blood from my nose, and I felt coldly furious. "I am going to get rid of you," I told my snakes. I had promised not to set the king snakes against the others, and I wouldn't. It wasn't a good idea anyhow. But there had to be another way.

Go ahead, said the scarlet king snake, and all the

others gave a hissy titter, **sss-sss-sss**. They didn't act like I was scaring them. Not at all. They seemed completely sure I couldn't do it.

Or maybe they knew something I didn't.

SIX

Tuesday morning I watched from the apartment window as Mom waited for her bus—she was going to a Humane Society committee meeting, I think. Anyway, the minute the bus drove away with her in it, I pulled on my blue crushed-velvet hat, ignoring a number of hissy complaints from my head, and headed out. I had some money, thanks to a guilt gift from Aunt Stheno because she hadn't sent me the hats, so I treated myself to a taxi. I told the driver, "NYU Medical Center."

I still thought maybe I could do something . . .

"Troy Lindquist," I told the woman at the visitor's information desk.

Troy Lindquissst. The scarlet king snake mimicked me.

"He is not allowed any visitors," said the receptionist.

I had figured it would be like that. I mean, everybody on the TV news was still speculating hysterically about mutant viruses and bioterrorism and whether there was going to be an epidemic of partial petrifications. I'd seen some people on the street wearing surgical masks to cover their mouths and noses.

I just nodded at the woman behind the desk. "I have a delivery for him." I'd bought roses, the sweetest-smelling kind I could find, from one of the vendors outside.

"Flowers? Take them up to the nurses' station on the fifth floor, west wing."

So I headed up there. But I didn't stop at the nurses' station. I strode past, into the west wing, trying to look like I worked there or something, like I did this every day of my life and I was busy and nobody better bother me.

It wasn't hard to find Troy. I just followed the crowd of white coats. No visitors? Ha. Maybe they weren't letting in kids Troy knew from school, but it looked like doctors had come from all over the country to have a look at the stone boy.

They were mostly men, taller than I am, talking medical stuff to each other right over the top of my head. They didn't notice me. I slipped between them and peeked in at the door first, to be sure it was Troy's room, and saw his stone Nikes and blue-jeans—well, white stone jeans now—at the bottom of the bed.

Forget having a few moments alone with him. It was standing room only in there. White coats everywhere.

But I had to try to help him.

There had to be something I could do . . .

Sssilly girl, grumbled the indigo snake. I don't undersssstand. Why not jusssst leave him?

Dusssie's half-human, said a corn snake kindly. She'sss concerned—

Ssso? That'sss her problem. We were jusssst doing our job—

Sssh! whimpered the yellow-bellied racer. I'm ssscared.

So was I. But I took a deep breath, let it out slowly, then started to edge through the whispering crowd in Troy's room, working my way to his bedside.

I caught glimpses between the white coats, seeing Troy in bits and pieces. Wires punched into the stone

of his arms and body, right through his stone clothing, wires leading to, like, TV screens. And tubes in
him leading to machines with plastic bags that put
liquids into him—the part that was still alive, I mean,
under the stone—or took liquids out of him, whatever. And his poor stone hands, up in the air rigid as
if he thought somebody was going to hit him. I saw
a stone Band-Aid on the web of his left thumb, like
he'd cut himself slicing a bagel. And when I saw
his face . . .

For a moment I felt weak. I had to stand still and
swallow hard.

It didn't matter that his eyes were no longer the
color of tarnished silver, that they stared at the ceiling
stony blind and white. He was still Troy, yet more
than Troy. I saw all the Prince Charmings of the
world in that marble face no human hand had
carved, perfect stone softness of brow and cheekbones and jaw and chin, perfect white marble blem-
ish on one side of his nose, his stone lips parted
slightly in—terror. He looked so scared.

I got myself moving again and wormed my way
between two nurses to lay the roses on the bed by his
head. Maybe he could smell them, I hoped. "Troy," I
told him softly, "it's me, Dusie."

Of course he couldn't say anything, or move, or even blink. There was no way for me to tell whether he could hear me, and if he did, whether he hated me. Whether he would want to put me in jail—

This was no time to start worrying about myself.

I bent close to his ear. "Troy," I whispered, "I don't know how, but I'm going to try to help—"

"Hey!" a man's voice boomed out behind me. "What's that girl doing in here?"

Somebody else ordered, "Get her out of here!"

I felt a nurse grab my arms.

"Wait!" yelled another man's voice. "Look at the heart monitor!"

A babble of voices broke out as I yanked myself free of the hands trying to pull me away from Troy.

"His heart's going like a racehorse!"

"His pulse is up to—"

"What's he reacting to?"

"The girl! What did—"

Quickly, before they could pull me away again, I bent and kissed Troy on his slightly parted lips, thinking Troy, Troy, wake up . . . I could feel a warm breath gasping in his mouth, but his lips felt so hard, so cold. Stone.

And they stayed that way. All that happened was

that the doctors kept yelling. "His body temperature just spiked!"

"His respiration's way up!"

"All his vital signs—"

I didn't care. Kissing him like he was Sleeping Beauty hadn't worked, so what now? Tell him I loved him and I would marry him, like in Beauty and the Beast? But no, I had it backwards, he was Beauty and I was the Beast, so he should tell *me*.

I couldn't think what to do. There was too much yelling.

"How could he feel that?"

"He didn't. She said something to him—"

"He heard her?"

"Young lady!" I felt a heavy hand on my arm. "What did you—"

I hate it when anybody lays a hand on me; it just flips me out. As Troy had discovered, poor guy. I snatched my arm away, and my snakes started to coil. Under its blue velvet hat, my head started to hiss. Voices inside my skull started to chorus worse than the voices in Troy's hospital room.

Predator!

Roussse! Roussse! Deploy necksss!

Deploy fangsss!

Prepare to ssstrike!

No! Ssslither away!

Essscape!

Good idea. Doctors and nurses grabbed at me from all directions.

Dusssie, essscape! urged the scarlet king snake.

I wrestled myself free and ran.

There was nothing else I could do.

Hanging onto my hat brim with both hands, I put my head down and scuttled between their legs like a—like a salamander or something. Sometimes being smaller has advantages. I scooted, I darted, I wormed and squirmed, I snaked right through the crowd in Troy's room and sprinted down the hallway. I jumped in front of some poor lady with a cart full of food trays and grabbed her elevator. The service elevator. I hit the close door button and the ground floor button and stood panting, trying to catch my breath, as the elevator lumbered down, down. It dumped me in the kitchen, and I took one look and ran for daylight. Out back of the hospital someplace, I dashed up a street, saw a bus pulling into a stop, and hopped on.

The bus rolled. I'd gotten away.

I slumped in a backseat for a long time, trying to

think, wondering whether Troy . . . had his heartbeat gone up because he liked me as a girl, the way those doctors seemed to think?

Or because he was terrified of me?

Did he know I was trying to help him?

Did he know I . . . I had no idea how to do it?

I guess my snakes knew I didn't want to talk, because they kept silent. They weren't so bad really, sometimes.

They stayed out of my hair, so to speak, while I got off the bus, caught another, and went home.

It was still morning.

Already I had failed.

≈ ≈ ≈

I ate lunch—leftover paella, leftover London broil, leftover General Tso's chicken, scrambled eggs, a can of tuna. I felt bummed, depressed, fat, fit to splat, yet I couldn't stop eating till I felt like I'd swallowed a pig.

Then I waddled to the sofa, where I collapsed and turned on the TV. I wanted to forget about my weird, messed-up life by watching cartoons or something, but the indigo snake commanded, *Sssnake show!*

And they all started yammering.

Sssnake man!
Python!
Boomssslang!
Sssidewinder!

"Oh, for God's sake," I complained. We'd caught a couple of segments of the animal channel the night before, that was my mistake. I was in no mood to watch any insane biologist dancing with reptiles. I whammed the power button to kill the TV, jumped up, yanked on my coat and an ugly head scarf, and slammed out.

I started walking with no idea where I was going. Thinking about Troy had me so bummed that even going nowhere felt better than sitting still. There was nothing much to see except chichi restaurants, big snooty art galleries, and expensive stores. And sky-scrapers in the distance, dark against a smoggy gray sky.

My mood was pretty dark and pretty gray, too. The air smelled of exhaust fumes and something rot-ting, maybe the Hudson River. I wished I'd thought to bring along my iPod so I could listen to music and not think. I wondered what Troy was thinking about me inside his stone skull. I wondered whether Troy's parents cried about him a lot. I wondered whether they visited him every day. I wondered whether they would keep him in the hospital or take him home and stand him in a corner. My snakes stopped hissing about the TV and went quiet, maybe rocked by the rhythm of my walking, maybe listening to my thoughts.

Sssome thingsss you can control, sssome thingsss you can't, said a gentle dandelion-yellow voice, a corn snake. *No ussse worrying.*

Like I said, sometimes they weren't so bad. "Corny," I grumbled, but I did feel better. Walking seemed to be a good idea.

Dusssie, said one of the little garter snakes, *tell usss a ssstory.*

"*Huh?*" What was this?

A ssstory! said several voices at once. Ribbon snakes, queen snakes, milk snakes.

The garter snake elaborated, *A ssstory about what it'sss like to have legsss.*

No! Tell usss about intessstinal parasssitesss, demanded a king snake.

Whoa. Who did they think I was, their mother? I was just a girl—well, I used to be just a girl—not a storyteller. "You tell *me* a story," I said, just to argue.

For once they all shut up; there was a silence in my mind. I walked aimlessly, watching the wind scuttle scraps of paper along the gutters like white rats, feeling so clueless that I guess my snakes sensed it. In a moment, a voice said, Very well. I will tell usss all a ssstory.

It was the smooth green snake, which was a surprise, to me at least. She hardly ever said anything.

She continued, I will tell usss the ssstory of the Ssserpent Mother and the Jewel of Wisssdom.

And she did. But I can't even begin to tell it the way she did, because I don't remember any words at all, just—just story, with colors that had fragrance and smells that sang and flickering tastes brighter than any dream:

A sun snake-ray flew to Mother Serpent and told her to go into the dark place. Back then snakes could fly, because they lived in the sky, rain snakes and wind snakes and the white-fire serpent of lightning and many others. But Mother Serpent was the first to crawl on the earth. She could fly without wings and run without legs, but now she had to venture into the dark. Why? she asked, and the sun snake told her: to find wisdom for the world.

She did not understand, but she obeyed. She burrowed down through sharp rocks that battered her bright scales. She burrowed through groping willow roots that tried to grab her. She became weak with hunger, for there was nothing to eat. She burrowed through masses of attack worms. Then when she got to the center of the earth she found a Wyrm, which was worse, a kind of giant worm dragon, coiled in the mouth of the World Tree.

The Mother Serpent smelled the presence of Wyrm with her forked tongue. She told him, I have come for Wisdom. No, he told her, you will never be wise. She told him again, I have come for Wisdom. He dared her, saying, Take it from me if you can. She anchored herself with a coil and reared her hard body to its full height and swelled her muscles and flattened her neck and hissed, Give me Wisssdom. And Wyrm told her, bite your tail, worm.

Now to call a serpent a worm is the greatest insult. So Mother Serpent knew she had to battle him, and she knew that it was as he had said, she was not wise and she never would be, for she knew Wyrm would kill her.

So they battled, and he did. He sank his fiery fangs deep into her head, blinding her, and shook her until her spine snapped, and flung her far away. She dragged her broken body out of the dark place, and when she felt the rays of the sun she stopped, and laid many moon-round eggs, and then she died.

The sun serpents kept the eggs warm. And out of them hatched many serpents, tree boas and sea serpents and adders and glass snakes and side-winders and anacondas and little striped garter snakes and many, many more, all the serpents of the world. And they crawled the earth, for none of them could fly, but each of them bore between its eyes a singular jewel, sapphire or ruby or topaz or emerald or amethyst, as befit the First Serpents of Earth. They all slipped through the great rib arches of the Mother Serpent's body, then slithered away north and south and east and west. The first humans saw the First Serpents, and coveted the jewels between their eyes, and tried to kill them. And many humans died trying. Some snakes died also, but many lived, and mated and laid eggs and gave more serpents to the world.

As time and generations passed, the jewel could no longer be seen, but all serpents bear it still between their eyes, within their minds, and the name of that jewel is Wisdom. And to this day, humans still hate and fear serpents and try to kill them, although they have forgotten why.

That was the story the green snake told. After it was over, there was silence. I kept walking till the gray sky over the city turned even darker. But my mind no longer felt dark and gray. The story gave me an awesome feeling that stayed with me for hours afterward, like Eternity perfume.

≈ ≈ ≈

". . . startling development in the Troy Lindquist case," the TV reporter said.

Halfway listening from my bedroom as Mom watched the news, I mumbled, "Uh-oh."

". . . when a mystery girl somehow bypassed hospital security, entered the stone boy's room, and kissed him," the anchorman was saying. "He responded . . ."

Mom yelled, "Dusie!"

I didn't move or answer.

". . . markedly elevated heartbeat, respiration, blood pressure, and brain activity." The anchorman sounded smug, like this was supposed to make people chuckle. "Doctors are no longer in any doubt that Troy Lindquist has intact hearing and can react to external stimuli. The mystery girl, however, vanished in the confusion. Witnesses remember only that she was wearing a large blue velvet hat . . ."

Mom screamed, "Dusie *Gorgon!*"

SEVEN

M om took away my blue velvet hat and made me
absolutely promise not to go see Troy anymore.

So I knew I couldn't.

It wasn't like I had any idea what to do for him
anyway.

Days kept going by.

Taking their good old time.

I felt so bummed.

And sooo bored. I kept my cell phone turned off
because I couldn't stand lying to my friends—they
had started asking what was wrong with me. I'd
returned my books to the library and looked for
more and read them and I still hadn't found a way to
get rid of my snakes. A person gets tired of television
even if she doesn't have snakes on her head who

want to watch boa constrictors like they're soap opera stars. I couldn't listen to my favorite music because my snakes complained in my head worse than static on a weak radio station. I couldn't get on the computer because Mom wouldn't tell me the password. She did not want me surfing the Internet unless she was home, which she hardly ever was. Even with all the volunteer work she did and the meetings she went to, I wondered where the heck she went all day, since she obviously wasn't at her so-called studio sculpting great art. I felt like she was avoiding me, and that gave me another thing to resent. It never once dawned on me that maybe, yes, okay, she was staying away from me, but it was because she didn't want me to see her crying.

So I spent most of the time alone and bored and feeling sorry for myself. Finally I started walking. For hours. Every day. Partly because I felt like I was fat and needed the exercise, partly because there was nothing else to do, but mostly because walking seemed to make me feel a little better.

After the first two days I got sick of SoHo and I took the subway to explore other places. South Street Seaport, Battery Park. Little Italy. Chinatown. Chelsea, with its wrought-iron fences and sunken gardens and all kinds of dogs walking their people. Greenwich Village. Specifically, Washington Square Park.

I didn't have to take the subway; I walked there. It wasn't that far away, and it was a sunny afternoon, with just a whiff of a breeze. Aside from a few winos I had to step over, Washington Square Park was cool. The NYU students dressed to be noticed. I was wearing my pink-and-yellow madras hippie hat and I fit right in. Street musicians played all around the park—my snakes didn't mind *their* music—a mime kept running into invisible obstacles, and a team of jugglers kept six wooden swords in the air at once, and there was a modern dance troupe in purple outfits and orange body paint trying to present something under the triumphal arch.

Let usss sssee! demanded a black racer, picking up the images from my mind.

Oh, God.

Sure enough, just like I was running a preschool, the rest of them started in. *We want to sssee, too! Sssee them dance! Dance like cobrasss! Let usss sssee, too!*

I felt little heads starting to poke out from under my hat.

"Stop it," I ordered between my teeth, walking away from the dance troupe and tugging down on the brim of my hat with both hands.

Dusssie, remove thisss absssurd headgear, ordered the scarlet king snake.

"Choke and die," I told her.

I'll bite your ssscalp!

"I'm sure I can find a freezer around here somewhere. You promised not to bite, remember?" Like me, they seemed to know they had to keep their promises. I glanced around to see whether anybody noticed that I was talking to myself and my hat was moving. But, duh, no problem. This was New York. Just like in midtown, people hurried by, barely noticing the violinists or the mimes or the dancers or me. All kinds of people. Guys in suits, businesswomen in fur coats and cross trainers, people with dreadlocks, hospital workers in scrubs, tweedy people who might have been professors, people in military uniforms, bag ladies pushing shopping carts, street people and commuters and kids and old people—I was keeping an eye out for the old man, what was his name? Cy, because he had said he went to NYU, but I didn't see him. Maybe it was too cold for him.

My snakes settled down and coiled close to my head for warmth. It got even colder, and darker, almost nighttime. The square swarmed with taxicabs, their white lights blinking on like they were big glowworms. People hurried even more, wanting to get home. It was time for me to get home, too. I sighed and headed down a narrow street toward SoHo.

Once I got away from the park, the neighborhood changed. No bistros, no shops, just apartment buildings, with almost nobody on the street. It wasn't a bad neighborhood, but it spooked me to be all alone. I walked faster, staying alert.

It'sss okay to be ssscared, whispered my yellow-bellied racer, his voice all green and worried. Unlike the other racers, he seemed to make being ssscared his ssspecialty. But he had picked a good time for it. On my head I heard other snakes start to hiss softly.

"Shush," I told them. "There's nobody around." Except about a block ahead of me was one other person, his back to me, an old guy with a funny bent-over, bow-legged walk. Because I'd never seen him from the back, I didn't recognize him till he paused under a street lamp and raised his head like a turtle to look around.

"Cy!" I blurted.

Too far away to hear me, he lowered his head and limped on. I smiled and started to trot to catch up to him.

But just as he stepped into the shadows before the next streetlight, somebody grabbed him.

An arm darted seemingly from the wall of a building, snatched Cy by the elbow, and yanked him out of sight.

I gasped and lunged into a run, sprinting toward where I had seen him. If there had been a car or anything coming at the intersection, it would have creamed me, because I didn't even look, just ran across. Halfway up the next block, I saw the alley, and in the shadows a cluster of street punks in do-rags and hip-hop pants. Among them I could hear Cy's sunny voice. ". . . boys want to rob people?" he was saying without a trace of anything except kindness in his tone. "Why? You're young. You could—"

"Shut up!" one of them snarled. "Give us your money, old man. Now!"

"I can't. Wouldn't be right. I'd be helping to corrupt you youngsters—"

They yelled, cursed, and there was a sick, smacking noise, and Cy gave a cry—they'd hit him. His cry went through me like getting struck by lightning. There was no time to think, only react. I screamed, "Stop it!" and my snakes hissed like a hive of dragons and reared, striking the inside of my hat as I snatched it off. Snakes bared, I charged, yelling "Stop it! Let him alone! Slimeballs, stop it or I'll . . ."

As the punks turned on me, I saw Cy fall, hitting the stony pavement with his frail old arms flung out, and it took all the control I never knew I had, every spark of willpower in my mind, to keep myself from giving them the glare that could kill them. Thank God I only had to hold myself back for an instant. They saw what I was, saw twenty-seven snakes on my head with their pale mouths wide open, striking and hissing and spitting. And those punks froze and went so white that they actually seemed to petrify for a moment before they ran like—

"Cockroaches!" I yelled after them, fists clenched. That was the way they ran, like cockroaches, like I'd flipped the light on. "Scumbugs!"

Then I heard a small, painful sound behind me and spun around, all my anger gone in a moment like water down the drain. "Cy! Cy, are you all right?"

He lay on the pavement hugging his one arm with the other and staring up at me with wide-eyed wonder, like I was the most amazing birthday surprise. "Well, I never," he murmured.

"Cy." I folded to my knees beside him, starting to shake. The sound of hissing whispered away as my snakes relaxed. The milk snake draped his checkered belly across my nose. I lifted him gently back to where he belonged, because I needed to see. "Cy, is your arm hurt?"

He barely seemed to hear me. "Well, I never in all my born days," he murmured, gazing at my head and smiling like an angel. "You *are* a doozy."

Then it hit me. Panic, I mean. I gasped, "Cy, please don't tell. Please, don't." I wasn't worried about the others, the street punks, because they'd never admit that a girl scared them, and even if they did talk about me and my snakes, nobody would believe them. But— "Cy, if people find out . . ." I started to cry. I couldn't help it. I sobbed, "They'll lock me up and—"

"Shhh. Dusie, it'll be all right." He reached out with his good hand and patted my knee.

"But—"

"I won't tell a soul about your beautiful, vehement snakes. I promise."

"But your arm—if it's broken—" I was bawling so hard I couldn't make sense, but I had my cell phone out, switching it on, so he knew I was thinking we should call an ambulance, and then there would be cops, too, and everybody would want to know all about it.

"Not at all, Dusie," he said in the most soothing voice. "Just help me up, if you would. Better find your hat first."

So I did. I couldn't stop crying, but I turned my cell phone off again, put it in my pocket, and got moving. I jammed my hat back on, then helped Cy up. It was like lifting a person made of dry sticks and Styrofoam, he was so light. On his feet, he stood unsteadily, still hugging his right arm with his left hand. I made myself calm down. "We'd better get you to a doctor," I said.

"I'll go to my own doctor. In the morning."

"But—"

"Could you walk me home, Dusie? I can walk, if we take it slow. Just keep me company, that's my girl. And please, tell me how you got your snakes."

So I did. As we slowfooted along the dark streets I told him the whole story, because he wanted to know and because having him by me felt so good. I'd never had a grandfather, but talking to him, I felt like now I did. I told him about waking up with the worst bad hair day of all time. I told him what I'd found out about my mother. I told him about meeting the Sisterhood in Central Park. I even told him I could hear my snakes thinking in my head. I told him—well, I told him everything. Even about Troy.

"I heard about that boy on the news. So *that's* what happened to him!" Cy murmured.

"It's all my fault," I said. My crying had quieted as we walked and I talked, but now I start sniffling again.

"Not at all," he said firmly. "It was an accident."

"But if I told the hospital or anybody—"

"Better not do that. I agree with your mother; they would not understand. Officialdom lacks imagination."

"But I feel like a criminal."

"You're not." He hobbled along clutching his hurt arm, his face tight with pain, yet he was able to give me a look like a blessing. "Dusie, you're a nice girl with your heart in the right place, and as far as I'm concerned, you're a hero. You saved my life. Those boys would have killed me."

I shivered. "You should have just given them your wallet."

"I couldn't do that."

"Why not?"

"It wouldn't be right."

"But—"

"I know, I know. But I'm eighty-seven years old. If I can't stand up for what's right by now, when can I?"

"You're crazy," I told him.

"Most of my friends would agree with you." He tried to smile, but winced with pain.

"We ought to get you a taxi," I said. "Or an ambulance."

"It's not far now."

His apartment was only a block down the street from mine. He fished his keys out of his pocket, but his hand shook, and he let me open the door. Inside, he collapsed in a chair. That's all there was, one big old recliner and a table with a lamp and a radio. The rest was all books, shelves and shelves and piles and piles of books. Books towering on the sofa, books stacked on the countertops in the tiny kitchen.

"Where's the phone?" I asked. "We should call somebody."

"There's nobody to call, Dusie."

"You don't have kids around here?"

"My children predeceased me. If you can help me rig up a sling, I'll be fine."

I barely heard him, because I was figuring out that he'd had kids but they were dead, that was what predeceased meant. Ow. Owww, that must have hurt. I said, "We should call your doctor, at least."

"You can try. The telephone is by the microwave."

I wondered whether there were books in the nuker, too. I found the cordless phone in its cradle behind a pile of Rudyard Kipling novels, along with a notepad, a pencil cup, and a list of emergency phone numbers. He was organized enough. I noticed the books were kind of stacked by topic or author. Robert Frost in the refrigerator, maybe, and Robert Burns in the oven. I dialed the doctor and got the answering service; an operator said she'd have the doctor call back.

I found the bathroom—yeah, he had stacks of books in there, too, all along the walls and around the toilet—and I grabbed a big, thin beach towel for a sling. Cy chatted with me while I eased it under his arm and tied it behind his neck. "So your mother is Euryale Gorgon. The sculptor." He sounded a bit dazed, as if too much had happened too fast.

"Right," I said, even though I'd already told him how the stone people had *so* not been carved.

But he kept talking like Mom was a real sculptor. "She's the one who did the statue in the Whitney—what's the name of it?"

"The man standing in the lobby? *Beyond.*" Although I had no idea why that was its name. Artists were expected to give weird names to their stuff.

"Yes!" Cy sounded excited that I knew what he was talking about. "*Beyond.* What a masterly work of art. Totally detailed and individual, yet you can't tell whether the subject is black or white or Asian or aboriginal or—or any other ethnicity. He can't be pigeonholed. He's Everyman. And the expression on his face . . . all the sorrow and joy and longing and love of the whole world."

"Um, I'm glad you like it."

"I'm dying to meet your mother," Cy said, "but I believe I'm a bit frightened of her."

So was I, but I wouldn't admit it. "Because she's a gorgon?"

"Because she's a genius."

"But, Cy, she's . . ." But my voice choked when I tried to say she was a fake, and all of a sudden I felt like Mom *was* a genius just by surviving, and kind of an artist just by—by being?

Could a life be a work of art?

Whatever, because just then the phone rang.

It was the doctor calling back. I brought Cy the phone, and he made an appointment to be at the hospital for an X-ray at six in the morning. I wrote stuff down on the notepad for him. After he beeped the phone off he told me, "Dusie, I'll be fine. I promise."

He wanted me to go home now, but he was too polite to say so.

"Don't you need some help getting to bed?" I asked.

"I'll stay right here. Just turn on the radio for me, Dusie, if you would."

I must have looked at him sideways, because he added, "I often spend the night here with my radio." He tilted the recliner back. "I've gotten too old to sleep much."

Okay, he looked about as comfortable as he was likely to get with a broken arm. I turned his music on for him—it was jazz. Then I wrote one more thing on the notepad. "Cy," I told him, "here's my number." I left it beside the cordless phone. "If you need anything, you call me."

"Yes, ma'am," he said.

"I mean it. You call me. Promise?"

He smiled wide and warm. "Okay, Dusie. You sleep tight and don't let the bedbugs bite, now."

Cy isss sssweet, remarked a corn snake, his thought tasting like sunrise and dew.

Cy isss nice, agreed a garter snake.

You guys are right for once, I thought as I let myself out of Cy's apartment.

"Dusie," he called after me, "I'll be absolutely all right. Don't worry."

But I did worry. All the way home and then some.

EIGHT

Mom was waiting for me, all dressed up in washable silk as usual, silk boots, silk turban, looking hissy enough to spit. "Dusie, it's almost bedtime! Why didn't you have your cell phone turned on? I called and called. Where have you *been*?"

"Nowhere." I felt real mixed up about everything, and I didn't want to talk to her.

"What do you mean, nowhere? You must have been somewhere."

"Nowhere in particular."

"Dusie Gorgon, did you go back to see that boy in the hospital?"

"No!" I started to get mad. Mom ought to know I keep my promises.

"Good," she said. "Then where were you?"

"It doesn't matter."

"Yes, it does! I want to know—"

"Why?"

She actually stamped her foot, and I noticed her turban was moving. When I was a little kid, Mom always used to hold down her turban with both hands when she got mad, and now I knew why. Her turban jumped as she yelled, "Because I worry about you!"

"What for?"

"All the things mothers *usually* worry about!" Her voice had gone about an octave higher than usual, and her turban was practically dancing. But my snakes stayed oddly quiet. They didn't hiss. They didn't mutter Predator. They didn't seem to want to diss my mother at all.

Mom raved on. "I worry that you're depressed, unhappy. I worry that you're at some unsupervised party drinking liquor or doing drugs. I worry that you've run away with some boy—"

"Ha," I said. "That'll be the day." I could just see me getting all kissy-face with some boy as he patted my snakes. Right.

Mom said, "Dusie, you're so *different* all of a sudden." Everything about her went slack and quiet within a moment. She said almost in a whisper,

"You're so *hard*. You don't let me *in* anymore. I don't know what's going on."

"Nothing's going on."

With her voice wavering a little she said, "I was worried you might have jumped off a bridge."

She was being stupid, yet that quiver in her voice made my heart hurt so bad I wanted to cry on her shoulder. But at the same time I felt mad enough to scream, because everything was all her fault, obviously. Why did she have to be a gorgon?

Like she could hear me thinking she said, "I know it's hard, but honey, I've been through the same thing. Let me help you. Please."

"Oh, get over yourself!" I turned my back on her, went to my room, and whammed the door shut. Too late I realized I was starving, but my pride wouldn't let me go back out once I'd slammed the door. I didn't get any supper that night.

≈ ≈ ≈

The next morning I made up for it by eating a huge breakfast. Two bowls of granola and then I went through the fridge like a vacuum cleaner. I ate cold chicken cordon bleu, cold stromboli, a jar of bacon

bits, cold rice pilaf, a block of Philadelphia brand
cream cheese, cold stuffed pasta shells with spicy Ital-
ian sausage, and some other leftovers I didn't even
recognize. Mom walked in and out of the kitchen
where I was having my feeding frenzy. She looked
at me sometimes, but she was real quiet. Well, so
what. It was morning. Nobody wants to talk in the
morning.

Sssome of usss do, remarked the pine woods snake.

Turtle eggsss? asked a king snake. *Dusssie, how about
sssome turtle eggsss?*

Or nice fresh sssalamandersss? begged a garter snake.

"Ew!" I managed to make myself stop eating,
grabbed a floppy hat, and left without yelling good-
bye to Mom.

I headed straight to Cy's apartment. It wasn't
much later than eight in the morning when I rang
his doorbell. But he didn't answer.

Okay, I told myself, he's okay. Probably he was
still at the hospital getting his X-ray. I sat on the concrete steps of his apartment building to wait. "Brrr,"
I said to nobody in particular, because it was a chilly
day and under my butt the steps felt as cold as a vice-
principal's heart.

If you humansss would hibernate like sssensssible

creaturesss, you wouldn't have thessse problemsss, said the scarlet king snake, warm and mouthy under my hat.

Dusssie, whined a corn snake, *tell usss a ssstory.*

"We've been through this before, guys." I didn't feel like calling them creeps anymore. "I don't tell stories." But all of a sudden I thought of one that might interest them. "Wait a minute. Whoa. Wait. Oh, wow. Okay, I'll tell you the story of how the first woman and the first man got kicked out of the Garden of Eden."

I told it to them by talking but also in my mind, trying to make pictures for them in my head, and I don't know how well I did, because I'm, like, a city girl. I'd never been anyplace very Edenish. I pictured the Garden kind of like Central Park if you let the Bronx Zoo loose in it. But I guess I did okay, because the snakes were quiet, taking it in, as I told about God making Adam and Eve out of clay. I imagined God as real old like Cy but a lot stronger, and Adam as kind of Troy grown up with a beard, and I should have gone straight on to Eve, but I had a stray thought about Adam naming the animals—

What namesss? demanded a king snake, interrupting.

"Huh?"

What sssort of namesss? Now it was a chorus. Milk snakes, racers, the indigo snake, all of them.

I didn't see what the big deal was. Like talking to kindergarteners, I said, "If it was a cat, he named it 'cat.' If—"

The smooth green snake interrupted. **Did he name me Opheodrysss vernalisss vernalisss or Eassstern Sssmooth Green Sssnake or Cricket-Hunter or sssserpent or just sssnake?**

"Oh. Um, I really don't know. Just snake, I guess. Can we get back to the story?"

I kept it up with the pictures in my mind as I told them how animals weren't enough company for Adam, so God made Eve. Okay, I guess I imagined Eve as a lot like me, only with hair instead of snakes. Anyway, the Tree of the Fruit of the Knowledge of Good and Evil was kind of a World Tree with all kinds of fruit on it and all kinds of birds in it. I'd got my idea of the World Tree from the story the smooth green snake had showed us. And the devil tempting Eve was a huge serpent spiraled around the trunk of the World Tree. I tried to make him mud-brown and ugly but somehow he ended up rainbow striped, all colors, kind of iridescent, with a blunt, handsome snaky face and human eyes. He said, "Eve, eat this,

and you'll know everything," and she was like Cy
with all his books, hungry to know the whole world,
not just Eden. So she did, she ate the fruit, which was
a banana, don't ask me why, and she was nice enough
to share with Adam. Then for some reason they
wanted to stop being naked and put clothes on. I
didn't know what fig leaves looked like, so the birds
flew down from the World Tree and gave them feathers to wear. Then God got all bent out of shape
because they were messing with the way he'd organized things, and the angel with the flaming sword
chased them out of the Garden, and that was why
people were supposed to hate snakes, because a snake
got them kicked out of Eden.

The story was over, but Cy wasn't home yet.

But the ssserpent gave them knowledge and wisssdom,
complained one of my black racers in a rainy blue
tone. *What'sss the problem?*

"They did what God said not to."

Ssserpents don't alwaysss do what they're told.

I didn't answer, because I saw a taxicab coming.

Eden sssounds like bassssking in the sssun, said the
corn snake who had started me telling the story. *Nice
at firssst, but then boring.*

The taxicab pulled up to the curb, and Cy got

out, smiling at me like neon, his clothes rumpled but the brand-new cast on his arm looking all starchy and white. "I stopped at the library," he said to explain why he was late. And here came the taxicab driver with an armload of books. On herpetology.

All formal like a diplomat Cy said, "Dusie, if you will permit me, I would like to offer you my assistance in the matter of the snakes."

≈ ≈ ≈

"What was it the Sphinx said again?" Cy asked me.

"Um, to lose my snakes I had to win, and to win I had to loosen. Or something like that." Sitting at his table with him, I watched him reading some humongous book on mythology. "Do you know what it means?"

He shook his head. "You?"

"I have no clue."

The corners of his eyes crinkled like he'd thought of a joke. "But Dusie, it says here that women with serpents for hair have magical powers and are full of wisdom and guile."

"What's guile?"

"Smarts. Like Odysseus had. The Greeks admired

brains. Their goddess of wisdom, Athena . . ." But then Cy frowned. "On the other hand, almost all their monsters were women. I can't make much sense of this."

No wonder. I got bored just looking at him trying to read it.

"Cy," I asked, "were you married?"

He glanced up from the fat book and smiled. "You know I had children. Three of them."

"Okay, stupid question." I mean, back when Cy was young, you probably *had* to get married to have kids. "How long were you married?"

"Forty-four years."

"Wow."

My snakes acted bored, too; maybe they were sleeping. Anyway, they were quiet on my head. I didn't have to wear a hat when I was with Cy, which was a relief. He liked to look at my snakes, studying them like a professor. Cy thought that if he learned enough about mythology or science or biochemistry or something, he could help me get rid of my snakes somehow. I felt kind of weirded out about the whole thing. I mean, I'd kind of gotten used to my snakes by then. But I liked it that Cy was trying to help me. But I didn't really hate my snakes anymore. But it

made sense that I had to get rid of them if I could. But I didn't think any of Cy's books would help.

But Cy did. He had it all planned out. First he would help me, and then he would concentrate on helping Troy. His reasoning was that if he helped me get rid of my snakes first, then when he cured Troy, there would be no incriminating evidence on my head in case Troy said something. Cy seemed absolutely sure he could rescue me *and* Troy if he just put his mind to it. I didn't really think he could, but I spent a lot of time at his apartment anyway, keeping him company and doing little things for him, like fastening buttons, opening a carton of milk or a bag of chips, dumb stuff that it's hard to do with a broken arm. His other friends, college kids, came to help him at night, but I had the day shift. I got to do his laundry. And open his mail for him. Stuff like that.

Just as I thought he'd forgotten I was there, he said, "It's been twenty years since Alina died."

"Your wife?"

"Yes."

"Were you in love?"

He gave me that glance again, wise and amused. "Hard to live with someone for forty-four years and not love them."

"Yes, but were you ever *in* love?"

"Oh, yes." His look got far away for a moment, then came back to me like a shot. "Do you worry about finding someone to love, Dusie?"

I felt myself blush. I mean, I hated to think it was that obvious. But yeah, even before the snakes, I'd always felt like I wasn't pretty enough or flirty enough or something. I mean, to get a boyfriend, it's all about clothes and clear skin and makeup and stuff, right? And hair. So, like, now . . . my heart felt so hollow that I managed to say the truth. "Nobody's ever going to love me with these snakes on my head."

Cy said, "I beg to differ. I am not even a herpetologist, Dusie, but if I were seventy years younger, I'd be on my knees to you this very moment."

I blushed so hard it felt like sunburn, and I blurted, "Why, for gosh sake?" But then, before he could answer, something happened that surprised me so much I forgot all about him. Inside my head a garter snake said in a small sunrise-pink voice, *We love you, Dusssie.*

Yesss, we do, said a blue racer.

And other snake voices spoke. *Jussst be yourssself*, said the smooth green snake who told stories.

We love you jussst the way you are, said the indigo snake.

We'll ssstick with you, said a milk snake.

Yeah, they were stuck with me, all right. As they spoke I caught a whiff of their green-smelling thoughts of how it might feel to be free snakes, wild snakes, complete snakes, snakes with tails to shake, snakes with grass and leaves under their bellies, snakes with real meals—rodents, eggs, soft-shelled baby crayfish—sliding down their long gullets, snakes with pits to hibernate in, snakes with other snakes to mate with. They thought all this, yet they felt my hollow heart and they said to me, *We love you, Dusssie.*

Sounding kind of like a jewel of wisdom, rigid but shining, the queenly scarlet king snake spoke for the whole head. *Dusssie, we all love you.*

I sat stunned. I couldn't think what to do about them. Couldn't say a word.

NINE

The next morning Cy met me at his apartment door, smiling. "Dusie, I do believe I may have it licked."

"Have it licked?"

"Licked!" Cy repeated, his smile widening clear across his face. "I may have figured out how to get rid of your snakes."

Then my heart started pounding.

And all twenty-seven snakes coiled tense and quiet under my lavender posy-print sunbonnet.

"Here, I'll show you." Cy waved me into his apartment with his right arm, the one that wasn't in a sling.

I followed him inside, taking off my hat, and sat at the table, trying not to let myself think too much that if this worked, I could go back to having friends and being normal, maybe even someday finding a boyfriend . . .

Cy sat down across from me, gesturing with his good hand, all excited. "I've been working on this day and night," he said. "I didn't say anything to you before because I didn't want to get your hopes up."

"Working on what?"

"Okay." He leaned toward me in a teaching sort of way. "Let's start from the beginning. This riddle the Sphinx addressed to you, you win some, you lose some, whatever it was—"

"To lose I have to win, and to win I have to loosen."

Cy nodded. "I must say that it makes no sense to me at all. Sounds like personal poetry. I decided to disregard it."

I had a feeling he shouldn't do that, but I couldn't say anything, because I didn't know what the Sphinx was talking about, either.

Cy went on. "And after all my reading in mythology, the only thing that seemed certain was that the snakes cannot be cut off your head without exceedingly negative results."

"Right."

"My instinct is that the same would apply if one attempted to remove said snakes via surgery, cauterization, laser, acid, et cetera. I do not think we can risk any such methods. Do you follow so far, Dusie?"

"Sure."

Sure, whispered a king snake, all brown and thorny. Mostly, my snakes seemed bummed, listening without comment.

Cy went on. "So I began to focus on snakes as such, in scientific terms. In herpetology class I have been learning about the life cycle of snakes, and I began to think—you know I hold a doctorate in chemistry. I worked in pharmaceuticals for over forty years."

Geez, I didn't know. I'd never thought to ask. I mean, I'd never talked to old people much, and I'd kind of forgotten to think Cy might have had a life.

"So I've been up nights studying herpetological biochemistry," Cy said, "and here's my thinking: Your snakes are drawing their sustenance from your bloodstream, just like a fetus in the womb. But if I could come up with some sort of inhibitor that would affect their metabolism but not yours, it would cut the umbilical cord, so to speak. If they were no longer being fed, they could not go on living indefinitely. They would simply starve and die."

I felt my snakes grow even more intensely still, like the boa constrictors on TV when they're about to strike and coil. But my snakes didn't strike. Or speak. I felt only their silence.

"Once I got on the right track, it wasn't hard at all," Cy continued, all eager and happy like a terrier. "I just needed a few basic chemical compounds in the proper proportions, and an emulsifier, and voila, a herpetological metabolism inhibitor to be applied externally."

I should have cheered or something, I guess, but I just sat there.

He must have seen how blank I looked. He tried to explain. "You know, their scales are just outgrowths of their skin. They have to be able to flex, so under and between their scales is soft skin a lot like yours. Porous. So I formulated the metabolism inhibitor as a kind of—you could call it snake lotion. Here it is. Look." He held out a glass mayonnaise jar full of greenish goo. "You just dab some of this on them."

Everything was happening so fast that I just stared at the jar in Cy's hand.

"Rather," Cy added, "on one of them. We ought to start with just one until we're sure it works as expected and that it has no adverse side effects on you."

I tried to think which snake I would want to kill. Not any of the king snakes. I couldn't help admiring them because they were so bold, their markings, their personalities. But not the timid garter snakes either, or the shy, pretty ribbon snakes, or the little queen snakes. And not the corn snakes, so kind, always trying to encourage me. Or the smooth green snake, the storyteller. Or my beautiful, bossy indigo snake, or my fraidy-snake yellow-bellied racer, or my pure amber pine woods snake, or . . .

Or any of them.

I felt my heart shrink. "Cy," I whispered, "I don't know about this."

"I'm almost certain it won't hurt you, Dusie."

"It's not that." I tried to look at him, but I had to stare at the tablecloth instead. I had been thinking about sneaking my snakes into the reptile house at the Bronx Zoo, so they could ogle the pythons and stuff. I had been thinking how I would help them peel off their old skins when it was time for them to shed, and how their new scales would shine. I had been trying to think of some other stories they might enjoy, like, a snake who put his tail in his mouth and rolled like a wheel, something like that. What I couldn't figure out was how to explain any of this to Cy. Finally I mumbled, "I don't really hate my snakes anymore. I kind of like some of them."

"You've started to think of them as pets?"

"I, um . . ." Maybe. I didn't know. I'd never had any pets except a goldfish.

"Well, that's very natural, Dusie, but you can't go getting sentimental about them." Cy reached across the table and touched my hand to make me look at him. Very serious, he said to me, "Your future is at stake."

"I know."

"I've tried to keep an optimistic outlook, but truly, you will not be able to live any sort of normal life with snakes on your head."

He was right, of course.

"Let alone any question of what happened to that Lindquist boy."

Oh, my God, what I'd done to Troy must never happen again. Never to anyone else. Never ever.

I knew I had to get rid of the snakes.

I knew I had to choose one of them to start with.

But at the same time my mind was thrashing around like a drowning person, and my snakes were so, so quiet. Guys? I appealed to them inside my head. Are you there? I need . . .

I needed their advice, which was pretty ridiculous, asking my snakes what I should do.

But, get this, they answered me.

We can't help you, Dusssie, said a corn snake in a voice like morning mist over a meadow, soft and golden.

Just as gently the indigo snake said, *Dusssie, you have to do what'sss right for you.*

There was a whisper of agreement from all of them. *Yesss. Yesss.*

We trussst you, said the milk snake.

In a cloud-white thought the scarlet king snake told me, *It'sss up to you, Dusssie.*

And a little garter snake said, *We all love you, Dusssie. No matter what.*

TEN

The rest of that day and into the evening I just sat on my bed staring at the jar of greenish stuff Cy had given me. I hadn't touched it other than to take it home and set it on my dresser, between my pile of hats and my Cinderella doll from F.A.O. Schwarz. Next to her the green goo looked disgusting. I shut myself in the bedroom with it, closed the door, and wished it had a lock, but I didn't open the jar of herpetological metabolism inhibitor. I just plopped on my bed, hugged my knees to my chin, and looked at it, trying to figure out what to do about my snakes . . .

Of course I need to get rid of them. Like Cy said, I'll have no future.

But the Sphinx has a career. And the others.

It's not like I want to be president or something.

What *do* I really want to do with my life?

I had no idea.

But then all of a sudden I did have an idea. I wanted to work with animals. Even though I had never even owned a pet, I wanted to be a veterinarian, or work for one. Or in a zoo or something. Or, I thought, maybe at an animal rescue shelter . . .

But that's crazy. All that hair and poop/pee/puke and stuff on my clothes and under my fingernails . . . If finding somebody to love was all about hair, makeup, and nice clothes, then how did people who do that kind of work, ever . . .

But obviously they did.

Maybe I was wrong about what it meant to "become a woman"? Or be a girl?

Or even to be human?

Or—or maybe being half-human meant I could be *more* instead of less?

Like, maybe, being different meant I should stop feeling sorry for myself and start thinking about what I could *do*? Such as, fight crime?

It wasn't my snakes giving me any of these ideas, either. My snakes were as quiet as daylight.

But nothing else in me was calm. My muscles ached and my skin sweated salty wet, yet my throat felt dry. My heart thumped. My thoughts flew back and forth like a Ping-Pong ball: I don't care! I don't want to be Super Snakewoman. I don't want to be a reptilehead and that's final. No, it isn't . . .

Do I really want to kill my snakes?

I don't want to be a cartoon character. I want to be normal, have a life—

But maybe I'm immortal . . .

So what. Do I want to be like my mother? Wait four thousand years for somebody to love me?

My chest hurt. My gut felt watery. My head ached and my brain started to churn like a washing machine, sloshing so hard I couldn't think. I mean, I had snakes on my mind in the most literal possible way, and all I wanted to do was crawl into a hole and hibernate until the whole thing went away. I wanted to stop thinking but I couldn't.

If I get rid of these snakes, does that mean I'm not immortal anymore? Will I get old and die?

I don't even know if I really am immortal.

What's the use of being immortal if I hate my life?

But maybe—like, look at Cy . . .

Cy had lost everybody he loved, yet he had a life and he still loved living. I could do that, too, I knew I could, especially if being half-human meant being more instead of being less. It would be a lot of work, but—

But nothing, I thought, and my anger came zinging back. I'd rather be dead.

Ping-pong went my brain: No, not really . . .

That's another thing, I thought, the snakes make me safe. If somebody tries to hurt me, I can scare them silly.

But what if I lose control? I don't want to petrify people, even partially. I don't want to hurt people.

So I want to kill my snakes?

No, what I really wanted to do was scream. My heart hurt. I felt bad all over. I mean, bad, as in, evil. Like the way I felt after I semipetrified Troy. Like this kind of thing shouldn't be happening, something was horribly wrong. Even my fingertips felt bad.

"Dusie?" Mom called when she got home.

I didn't answer her.

"Dusie, are you here?" She peeked into my room. "Oh, there you are." I could hear the relief in her voice. "What are you doing?"

Couldn't she see I was sitting on my bed staring at a jar of green goo? "Nothing, Mom."

"Do you want something to eat? We could order Thai food."

Thai food was my favorite, and she knew it. But I shook my head.

Mom went into her room and changed into her silk pj's and sleep turban. She came back in maybe half an hour.

"Dusie?"

I didn't answer.

"Dusie, aren't you hungry at all?"

"No."

"Honey, what's the matter?"

"Nothing."

"Come on, sweetie, what is it? Please tell me."

"Nothing! I'm okay, Mom."

She went away, and I sat there and stared at the green goo snake lotion until I wasn't seeing it anymore. Instead, I was looking inside myself, trying to negotiate some kind of deal between my befuddled head and my aching heart . . .

Do I need a special boyfriend to be happy?

Yes. I need somebody to love.

And to love me.

But who could love me when I have snakes on my head? What about me would anybody love?

Well, I suppose I'm kind of nice sometimes . . .

At that point I really felt like I was pretty much nothing but a monster. But then all of a sudden, after all their silence, my snakes spoke up.

Dusssie, ssstop that! the scarlet king snake burst out all fire colors, like lightning had struck.

I felt all my snakes rearing up on my head.

You're ssstrong, Dusssie! said another king snake.

You're sssweet, said all the corn snakes at once.

Nice. Gentle, said a milk snake, whispering like white dawn light.

You're bright, Dusssie! cried the ribbon snakes. *You're rainbow, like usss!*

You're brave, declared the black racers.

But it'sss okay to be ssscared sssometimes, added the yellow-bellied racer.

The black racers turned on him. *Shut up, you! Even when Dusssie's ssscared she'sss ssstill gallant.*

I interrupted. "Huh?" Gallant?

Gallant! Bold! Brave, like usss, to go sssee Troy, to sssave Cy.

Oh. Cy.

Okay, it was true, I could have run away instead of trying to help.

And I remembered what Cy had said. That I was a nice girl with my heart in the right place.

And it was true, that I wanted . . . I wanted good things for people. And I never wanted to hurt anyone.

We are your ssserpents, put in the indigo snake.

We are usss, said a green snake, *becaussse of you*.

Then they were all talking at once again. *No hog-nossse sssnakes on thisss head! No worm sssnakes! No ssslug sssnakes! No vipersss! Look at usss!*

I didn't have to. I knew. They were beautiful. Every bright yellow azure turquoise rings shining golden stripes one of them.

Ssso what are you? demanded the scarlet king snake.

"I'm—I'm Dusie."

But through their wild spines deep into the bone of my skull and right to the heart of my mind I knew some things now. I knew that my corn snakes were kind because I was. I knew that my king snakes were strong and bossy because I was. And my black racers were bold because I could be bold when I had to be. But also I was gentle like my milk snakes and timid like my yellow-bellied racer and shy like my garter snakes and sweet like my little queen snakes and . . . blue, bright, funny sunny storm night and day, all of it was in me. So much that didn't depend on a hairdo.

"Oh!" I whispered.

Oh. Oh, my gosh, I wanted to remember this moment forever.

Yet, I still had to kill them.

And it would feel like killing myself.

But what choice did I have?

≈ ≈ ≈

I was still in the same place, slumped on the bed, when Mom opened the door again. "Sweetie, are you sure you don't want something to eat?"

Something was making my throat choke up so I couldn't talk. I shook my head.

Mom opened the door wider and came into my room. For some reason she'd changed back into her street clothes, and not just any old outfit, either. She wore her best turban, crimson satin, and the rest of her was kind of draped and sashed and scarfed and shawled with crimson and gold and black and sequins and bugle beads and stuff. I guess if you were raised in ancient Greece, you knew how to wrap and drape.

She looked like she was going someplace important, and also, even to me, she looked way beautiful.

She said, "Okay, then come on, Dusie." It was an order, but a gentle one. She put out her hand to me like I was still a little kid. "Come with me," she said in the same way. "We're going out."

I stiffened and pulled away from her.

"Dusie, come on," she repeated. "I'm taking you to meet your father."

I think my breath stopped for a moment. I stared at her, and she stared back. She said, "It's the only thing I can think of that might help."

I didn't know whether it would help, but it was the only thing that could possibly have gotten me moving.

I got up and reached for the nearest hat, which was a silver taffeta one. I jammed it onto my head, tucked my snakes into it, and followed Mom out the door.

ELEVEN

We sat silent for what seemed like a very long subway ride. I just slumped and let myself get jounced around. Finally Mom touched my arm to tell me we were pulling into our stop, and I followed her off. At the top of the stairs I breathed deeply of the night air and looked around to see where we were.

Fifth Avenue. Mom turned uptown. We walked side by side along the edge of Central Park.

It took me a long time to work myself up to it, but eventually I asked, "Where are we going?"

Mom took a long look at me but didn't answer. In the streetlamp light I saw her mouth tweak into a Mona Lisa smile. She said, "You look a little like my sister Medusa."

Of all the times for her to get mysterious and annoying. "Wonderful," I grumped.

"Before Athena put the curse on her, I mean." She stared up Fifth Avenue. "And I will have you know that my sister Medusa was exquisitely lovely. Her beauty rivaled that of any goddess. That is why Athena grew jealous and angry, because Poseidon's eyes turned to my sister."

"Whatever." Why was she telling me all this ancient history?

"But guess what, Dusie?" Mom turned toward me again, looking for a response. When I just kept on walking, she kept on talking. "Even at the height of her beauty, when she bloomed like a rose, Medusa never felt truly loved. She had many sweethearts, but what if they loved her only for her fair face, her golden hair, her body, and not for herself? Do you see, Dusie?"

I could not keep a sullen edge out of my voice. "Are you telling me I should be grateful to be an ugly snakehead?"

"I am telling you there is little blessing in being loved for the sake of beauty."

I sighed, wondering how much worse things could get. Mom was supposed to be helping me with my problem but she was lecturing, and now I felt cramps deep in my gut. Great. Just wonderful. Had it been a month already? I glanced at the sky, all linty with stars. Yes, there was the new moon, a thin crescent that looked stuck, like, on a black tablecloth, as if a careless goddess had thrown a fingernail paring there.

"Athena was superlatively beautiful," my mother was saying, "but she did not feel sure of Poseidon's love. Medusa had sweethearts, but when Athena cursed her to make her ugly, they all left her."

"Well, snakes for hair," I burst out, "no wonder!"

"True. And it's no wonder, either, when a man falls in love with a pretty woman. But think of the greatness of the wonder when a man loves a gorgon."

Oh.

I started to get it, even though I didn't want to.

We walked another dark block before I managed to say, "Are we talking about my father?"

"Yes. There is love and then there is true love. There is the love of a man for a pretty woman, and then there is the kind of love your father gave to me."

"*Oh*," I breathed.

Now I was listening.

She started slowly to tell me about my father. "He was not an American." Past tense; was he dead?

"Maybe because of his native culture, he was very different than most American men. He was very intuitive. So intuitive that at times he seemed telepathic." She gave me a soft glance. "Maybe you get that from him."

"Huh?"

"Hearing your snakes talking."

I goggled at her. "So you believe me now?"

"I stopped sending you to doctors, didn't I?" Then she added more gently, "Yes, I believe you."

Yesss, whispered somebody on my head.

"Your father would have wanted me to believe you."

Yesss!

Shhh!

Lisssten.

"He was a remarkable man," my mother went on. "Most people didn't realize, because he looked ordinary and he did ordinary work, any kind of honest work he could get—but he himself wasn't ordinary. He was a magic man. A miracle man."

My snakes were very quiet, and so was I. Almost afraid to breathe, afraid she might change her mind and stop talking, I listened with my whole heart.

She told me how she and my father, when they first met, just talked and talked about art, theater, religion, philosophy, ways to change the world. How he had courted her with poetry, addressing his love to her soul. How he had waited a long time for her to learn to trust him.

At Seventy-fifth Street we turned away from Central Park. I am not sure when I began to know where we were going.

"He told me his secrets," said my mother. "For one thing, he was in this country illegally, and likely to be deported, and if that happened, if he was sent back to his home country, he would be tortured and killed."

Tortured. Killed. The words gave me a chill. If that had happened to him . . . but she would never have let that happen to him.

"And, in time," my mother went on, "I told him my secrets. All about me. Everything."

There it was. The Whitney Museum. And looking at us in the pale glow of the security lights, from behind the glass of the locked entrance, stood my mother's masterpiece, a life-size stone man, *Beyond.*

"Beyond belief," explained my mother softly. "My miracle man. Beyond understanding."

Sssee, Dusssie? whispered the scarlet king snake inside my head, and her thought smelled gentle and peach-colored, like sunrise. **Sssee?**

I saw. I had seen him before of course, but then I had not known it was my father who stood there with his soul in his stone-sculpture face—yearning, quizzical, tragic, quirky, and above all, loving. He gazed at me with such love that I started silently to cry, tears slipping down my cheeks.

Yesss, murmured a chorus of serpents, hushed, like dawn. **Yesss, you sssee.**

Yes. I did. Although I could not have put into words what it was that I saw. Or sensed, like catching a whiff of cinnamon on the breeze. Or heard echoing faintly from the horizon of my mind, like music from a wild wooden flute.

When I had taken a moment to think, I turned to my mother. "They came for him?" I asked. "The immigration people?"

"Yes. And his peaceful soul would not let me do this to them, not even to save him. So . . . he wanted it this way."

I gazed into his gentle stone eyes awhile longer, and when I glanced at Mom again, she was taking off her turban. And oh my God, the serpents on her head—they made my snakes look like pretty little hair ribbons by comparison. Rippling, muscled like weight lifters and thick as cables they reared their viper heads. I took a step back; I couldn't help it. But then I stood still and gazed, amazed: those serpents on my mother's head, every ugly one of them, swayed upward to stretch and yearn toward my father's beyond-this-world face.

≈ ≈ ≈

I waited around the corner to give my mother a little time alone with my father.

And to give me a little time alone with me. Dusie.

Deep in my belly I felt cramps crawling as if I might give birth to something.

I stared up at the sparkling dark sky.

Then Mom walked up to me, turban covering her head, her face as peaceful as moonlight.

I felt myself smile, looking at her. "Do you come here a lot?"

"Almost every day."

I nodded, then pointed up at the silver crescent of new moon in the sky. "Is that the maiden moon?"

She looked, and gasped. "I forgot!" she exclaimed. "The Sisterhood!"

TWELVE

By the time we got back to Central Park, the Sisterhood had already assembled. I heard a murmur of voices as Mom and I strode down the winding footpath, then silence when, I guess, they noticed our footsteps approaching. Stepping into the hollow between the three giant boulders, I looked around, blinking in the dim light—but these beings gave off their own luster. The Sphinx lay on her crag as before, her topaz eyes gleaming down at me, her great lion paws flexing so that the hooked claws slid in and out. A Lamia spread her dragon wings on top of another boulder, and on the third one—it had to be Siren, the one I hadn't met before, with a delicate angel face atop huge condor wings. On all of them glimmered a sheen more than just moonlight. Magic.

I knew I needed to be there, yet I started to sweat.

Then I saw others. Aunt Stheno stood beside my mom. Birdwomen—fates, furies, harpies?—perched all around, on rocks and trees and a few of them on the ground, too close to me. Nemesis, the one with ostrich feet, smiled at me as if she might eat me. I wanted to run. My heart hammered. I couldn't think.

Let usss sssee, Dusssie? whispered a garter snake.

I pulled my hat off, holding it in both hands as if I were hanging onto it for support, and it helped me think of something to say. Facing the lion woman with glittering wise eyes, I told her only a little shakily, "Thank you for the hats, Sphinx."

Deep in her silky throat she gave a growl—no, she chuckled. A murmur of surprise went around the Sisterhood. Out of the corner of my eye I saw my mother standing next to me, looking at me, wide-eyed. But my snakes, like me, had known for a while. I mean, it had to have been somebody who knew, somebody in the Sisterhood, and who else could read me like the Sphinx? Also, the Sphinx had connections on Broadway, with costume makers. So no big deal.

In her honey-dark voice the Sphinx told me,

"Good for you, young Gorgon. But have you yet found the answer to my riddle?"

She'sss ssso inssscrutible, murmured the smooth green snake, my storyteller.

And ssso golden, added a pine woods snake enviously.

"I—I'm not sure." Actually, since Cy had given me the green goo, I had forgotten about the Sphinx and her riddle. "You mean about getting rid of my snakes?"

"Assuredly, yes."

"Well, um, a lot has happened." Now that I had managed to start talking, I blundered on, because I felt like I ought to clear up some things with her and the Sisterhood. I mean, I'd sworn to them I was going to get rid of my snakes. "I've met a nice old man, a scientist, and he . . ." I felt my mother staring at me, which made it hard to concentrate, but I kept going. "He thinks it'll be okay if the snakes aren't cut off but just die on their own. And he's come up with a, um, a metabolism inhibitor medicine. If I put it on them, he believes they'll starve and die."

Several members of the Sisterhood gasped as if they had won the lottery. And my mother cried, "Dusie, how wonderful!"

Looking at the Sphinx was not easy, but at this point I found it better than looking at my mother. I kept talking as if I hadn't heard Mom. "But I've decided not to do it," I said.

"What?" My mother was not the only one who exclaimed.

"I don't want to kill them." My voice shook, but I had to say this. It was the answer I had found in my father's eyes. It was the only way that felt right. And it was the only way that was me. Dusie.

Dusssie, whispered all my snakes in a chorus that smelled like dew, glowed like sunrise. Our Dusssie.

"But why not?" Mom cried.

I said, "I love them."

Moon-white blank silence met me. Not one of those immortals said a word or made a sound, not even a sigh. I could hear only some nighttime traffic noises, bare tree branches scraping in the breeze, and the inside of my own mind, where my snakes were whispering my name over and over again, all rainbow colors. Dusssie. Dusssie!

The scarlet king snake told me, We knew we could trussst you.

"You love them," the Sphinx said with no more

emotion than the sound of a pebble dropping into a wishing well.

I knew I had to try to explain. "Not like pets," I started, remembering what Cy had said. "They're more than pets. They're my friends . . . no, they're closer than friends." They were even closer than family, although I didn't say that with Mom and Aunt Stheno standing there. "They're with me all the time. They make me be myself, not just what other people want me to be. They're part of me." What was it the scarlet king snake had said? "They're my thoughts. They're who I am. They're strong, so I'm strong, too, and I never knew I could be strong. And I never knew I could enjoy myself *by* myself. I never knew I could tell stories . . ." My voice kept gathering strength, because I was getting mad. Frustrated, really. All these freak women, they were so silent, and, like, how the heck was I supposed to explain love?

I took a step toward the Sphinx. "They're me but they're themselves, too. They're individuals. Look. This one is bossy, but she gives really good advice." I lifted a hand to my forehead, and the snake rested part of her belly in my palm. "This is my scarlet king snake—"

All of a sudden I felt like she needed a name. I mean, I was introducing her to the Sphinx.

But it had to be the right name for such a regal serpent.

I said, "This is my scarlet king snake, Regina."

There was a soft explosion of snake thought inside my mind, a joyful hissy seething, like a fountain bursting out of stone. And as the echo of her name still hung on the night air, my scarlet king snake, Regina, slipped across my hand and spiraled down my arm to rest her neck in my other hand. Flicking her golden forked tongue, she looked at me with her unblinking eyes.

I gawked at her. Regina, my queenly king snake. Red-black-yellow-black all the way down her four-foot-long body. Regina, the entire Regina, including tail, the works. All of her.

Dusssie, she thought to me, and even though she was a whole snake now, not a part of my head anymore, I could still hear her. *Dusssie, you have completed me.*

I stood, stunned.

Dusssie, she begged me, *the othersss. Ssset them free.*

I stood there like a major idiot, holding Regina, for at least a minute before I started to get it. Then

I looked at the Sphinx, and I managed to say, "To lose, I must win, and to win, I must loosen . . ."

The Sphinx didn't say a thing.

Regina told me, You've won our heartsss.

Oh. Oh, and they'd won mine too, but I knew I had to let them go. For their sakes. So that they could slip through the grass of Central Park and bask on the rocks and eat mice and minnows and find mates. I had to.

I swallowed hard, and bent to set Regina down on the ground, then lifted my hand to my head again. The first snake I touched happened to be one of my favorites, one of the corn snakes. It was easy to find the right name for him. "This is Sunshine," I said.

Again there was that soft explosion within my mind, like liquid fireworks. Then Sunshine, too, slipped across my hand and down my arm. Dusssie, he said as he left me, Dusssie, thank you. I love you.

I closed my eyes against tears and kept going. Sometimes I had to wait a minute for the name, because it had to be right, not just any name but the good and proper name for each snake. But the names kept coming to me like they were given by somebody smarter than me. Maybe the Sphinx was helping me. Or maybe I really was smart and just never knew it before. Whatever it was, the best names just kept coming to me. Like, for my smooth green snake: Scheherazade, after the storyteller in the Arabian nights. For the black racers, because they were so quick and bold: Zorro, Ebony Saber, Pirate. For the yellow-bellied racer: Lionel, because he was like a cowardly lion. For the bright-colored milk snake: Broadway.

"Snakes run without legs and swim without fins. Like spirits." Hearing in my mind that I wanted her next, the indigo snake met my hand. "This is my indigo snake, Spirit."

Ssspirit thanksss you, Dusssie. She slipped off my head, down my back, and away into the night.

"Snakes are wise," I murmured, wondering whether I would ever be as wise. I found a queen snake with my hand. "May I introduce—Solomon."

He darted down my arm and disappeared into the darkness.

I gave more wisdom names: Archimedes, Sibyl. Then I gave jewel names, for the jewel of wisdom they carried invisibly between their eyes. The blue racers, Lapis and Turquoise. The pine woods snake, Topaz. The two rough green snakes, Emerald Secret and Emerald Mystery.

The king snakes, because they were so strong, I named Hero and Gladiator. I didn't know how I was going to be strong without them, but I knew I had to try.

The little garter snakes I called Ripple, Streamline, Ribbon—I can't remember all the names. I gave more names, and more, and one by one my proud serpents arched their necks and left me. The very last one was a ribbon snake who had encircled my head like a crown. I unwound her with both hands. "Snakes do not hunt in packs. Snakes are often alone. May I introduce Solitaire," I said, my voice starting to sound ragged. And I lifted her away from my head, a whole snake now. Warm and quick she slipped down and away.

I stood there feeling kind of like a helium balloon. Weightless. Empty. Lightheaded.

Gone. My snakes were all gone, all twenty-seven of them.

I stood among my mother and many other women, yet I felt alone. Lonely.

"I'll miss you," I called to the night. Hard to believe, but after a month of wishing I could get rid of them, I already did miss them.

But from somewhere out there in the grass and

rustling leaves, in the damp spring-scented night, responses floated to my mind.

We misss you, too!

Come sssee usss, Dusssie!

Remember usss, Dusssie!

Remember, jussst be yourssself!

To win you mussst loossse, Dusssie!

And the clearest voice, Regina's, told me, *Dusssie, remember thisss: to find love, give love.*

THIRTEEN

Forget about sleeping that night.

I kind of lost track of time, what with the Sisterhood congratulating me and asking questions and exclaiming over my hair—I had the most amazing hair now, thick serpentine curls rippling down my back and shoulders, kind of arranged in coils by color. Basically it was different shades of shiny brown, but long spirals of it were wavy amber gold or ebony black or garnet red or yellow like garter snake stripes. Anyway, they loved my hair, and they wanted to know all about the snake metabolism inhibitor and we talked and talked. It must have been way after midnight when Mom and I headed home.

We treated ourselves to a taxi. Mom sat straight up in the backseat and—she wasn't smiling, exactly, but joy glowed like moonlight in her face. We didn't talk much, but I've never seen her look so happy.

"I am so proud of you," she said all of a sudden.

"What for? I didn't do anything." I mean, I felt good about what had happened—my snakes were free now and so was I—but I hadn't planned it that way, and my mind felt awfully quiet now that my twenty-seven best buddies were gone.

"For being who you are," Mom said. "One of a kind."

I opened my mouth to say that anybody could have done the same thing, but then I looked at her, still with snakes on her head after how many thousand years?

"I couldn't have done it," Mom said as if she knew exactly what I was thinking. "I could never learn to love these vipers. They're evil-tempered, venomous, hideous—"

But her snakes should match who she was. I burst out, "You're not like that!"

"I was," she said, matter-of-fact. "I was bitter, venomous, slug-ugly inside until your father loved me."

Oh.

"And then I had you." Mom gave me the most

amazing look: yearning, quizzical, tragic, quirky . . .
"And you changed me even more."

Oh. I just sat there hearing the taxi wheels swish
down Greene Street. I couldn't say a word, but I
reached over and touched her hand.

Next thing I remember, the taxi pulled up in
front of our apartment building. Then I guess we got
out, but I don't exactly recall walking inside. I felt
like I was floating, like all of me was filled with
helium now, not just my head. Mom still had that
moonlit look on her face. We kind of wafted through
the empty lobby—

"Dusie."

The low voice came from a corner behind the
potted miniature apricot tree at the entrance. I whirled
and stared. He took a couple of steps toward me, chin
down as he tried to smile, looking embarrassed.

And so beautiful. Especially the Band-Aid on his
thumb and the zit on the side of his nose.

And so not pissed at me. In his shy tarnished-
silver eyes I saw understanding.

And so *not* made of stone.

"Troy!" I screamed. I ran to him and threw my
arms around him, hugging him and hugging him. He

felt just the way a human being ought to feel, warm and solid, not semi-petrified. He hugged me back, but not too hard. Kind of like he was half scared of me.

My legs insisted on jumping, so I had to let go of him. "Troy," I yelled, bouncing on the lobby floor like it was a trampoline, "what are you *doing* here?"

"Um, last summer I found out where you lived," he said. "In case I ever got up the nerve to ask you for a date or something."

"Huh?" He wasn't making much sense. "No, I mean, you're okay again! How—"

"Oh. Yeah, that was pretty amazing." His voice went hushed. "A couple of hours ago, you did it, right? Mother Serpent said to me, *Young human hatchling, Medusa has triumphed. Shed your skin!* Then she turned all colors like a sunrise and grew white-fire wings and flew away. I wanted to fly, too. I jumped out of that stupid bed and yanked all the tubes and stuff out of myself and it didn't even hurt." He lifted his arms and ran his hands down them like he was checking for blood or holes, or something, but there wasn't a mark on him. "I felt so good I couldn't stay in that place another—"

Behind me a sunny old voice exclaimed, "Well, I never!"

I spun around and there in the lobby stood Cy, broken arm and all, with a big smile taking over his pale skinny face.

"Cy!" I hugged him.

"Don't knock me over! Well, I never in all my born days," he said, patting my shoulder as he looked from me to Troy and back again. "Dusie, your snakes—I mean, your hair—don't tell me the metabolism inhibitor—"

I felt so good I started laughing. I didn't even try to explain.

"This would be Troy Lindquist?" I felt Cy peering over my shoulder at him. "I was listening to my radio and I heard a news bulletin about you, young man, that you'd gone missing from the hospital—"

"Oh, crap," Troy muttered.

"And I kept trying to phone this young lady . . ." Cy patted my back. "She didn't answer, so I got worried—"

"I was hoping nobody would notice till morning," Troy said. "The hospital, I mean. Now they probably freaked out my parents. I'd better call home."

"You can use our phone." I started toward the elevator to lead the way to the apartment. "Come on, Cy, you come, too. Mom, gimme your key—Mom?"

There she stood like she barely heard me. Almost like I'd managed to turn *her* into stone somehow. Stiff with terror, all the joy gone from her face.

"Mom?" I stared at her. "Mom, what's the matter?"

But Troy understood right away, a lot quicker than I did. He said, "Mrs. Gorgon, it's okay." He touched her arm. Her eyes widened and shifted to look at him. He repeated, "It's okay. I won't ever tell anybody."

"Oh, Mom," I complained as I began to understand. As I saw relief dawn in her eyes.

Troy nodded. "I promise. I'll just say I woke up in the hospital and I don't remember how I got there. But actually . . ." Troy looked at me, his eyes like silver mirrors. "Actually I'll never forget the day you visited, Dusie," he said softly. "You told me it was gonna be okay, and I knew it would. And the Mother Serpent was with me the whole time . . ." He hesitated, his voice fumbling for words. "She had this jewel shining all colors between her eyes, and I saw, like, pictures in it. And she taught me things."

"Wisdom," I whispered.

"Or maybe craziness." He grinned at me. "Anyway, I'm not about to let anybody know about you, or your mom, or your aunt, or any of them. The

Sisterhood." He gave my mother a long, quiet look. "I promise."

And friends of the Mother Serpent, I knew, kept their promises.

"And you are absolutely not to worry about me, either." Cy shook hands with Mom. "Mrs. Gorgon, I'm honored to meet you, and I'd be delighted to offer you a supply of my herpetological metabolism inhibitor if you'd care to try it."

Mom blinked at Cy like she couldn't believe him. But then her Greek-statue face came back to life, and she smiled like a goddess hosting a dinner party. "You're *wonderful*, both of you." She glanced from Cy to Troy, her eyes shining like jewels. "Why are we standing in the lobby? Come on up to the apartment. I know a place that delivers the most wonderful Thai food. . . ."

Troy shook his head. "I'd better go. We don't want anybody to find me here."

Mom gave him a long look and nodded. "Please come back another time, then. Let me get you a taxi—"

"No need." He pulled a cell phone from his pocket. "If the battery's still okay after being turned to stone." He pushed a button with his thumb, and a light went on. He nodded. "I'll walk a couple of blocks, then call my parents. I'll be fine."

I told him, "Thanks, Troy."

"No problem. Good night, Mrs. Gorgon." But Troy looked at me as he headed toward the door, and his chin rose as his walk slowed down, and all of a sudden he acted soooo cool. "See you in school, Dusie?"

"Um, yeah. Sure." Wow, I could finally go back to school now.

Troy nodded. "Hey, I like the new hairdo," he teased just as he stepped out the door.

"Nice of you to notice!" I sang after him.

Mom grabbed me in a hug, laughing. She threw back her head, vipers coiling heavy in her turban, and laughed almost like a girl. And totally like a human being.